Justice Calling

The Twenty-Sided Sorceress: Book One

Annie Bellet

 Published by Doomed Muse Press.

Cover designed by Ravven (www.ravven.com)
Formatting by Polgarus Studio (www.polgarusstudio.com)
First edition, 2014

If you want to be notified when Annie Bellet's next novel is released and get free stories and occasional other goodies, please sign up for her mailing list by going to: http://tinyurl.com/anniebellet. Your email address will never be shared and you can unsubscribe at any time.

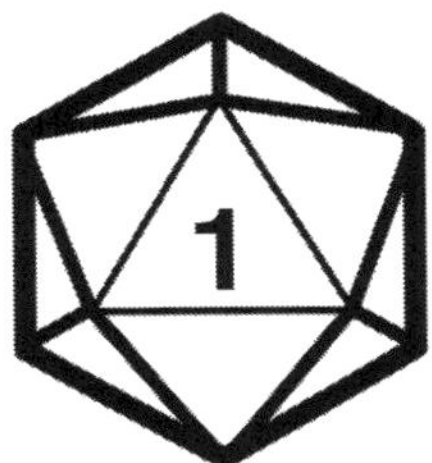

Life-changing moments are sneaky little bastards. Often we don't even know that nothing will ever be the same until long after, and only in hindsight can we look and say, "There! That was it! That changed everything."

Well, at least we could, if we're alive to do it.

For me, it was just another Thursday evening on a blustery spring day. I was finishing up a Japanese-to-English translation job and only somewhat pretending to mind the register in my comic and game shop. That's the benefit of being the owner, I suppose. No one was going to tell me to be cheerful and pay attention to customers.

There weren't any, anyway. Thursday nights are game night and we close early. I hadn't flipped the sign yet as I was waiting on Harper, my best friend of the last four years, to stop swearing at her game of StarCraft.

"No amount of Banelings in the world are going to save you here," I said, glancing over at her screen.

"Marines are overpowered," she growled.

"Sure," I said, trying not to laugh. It was an old gripe. Whatever race her opponent played in the game was always OP, according to the logic of Harper. "Maybe you should play with a mouse instead of just your trackpad?"

"I'm practicing my hotkeying," she said. "Shut up, you're distracting me."

The string of bells on the door tinkled and I turned away from my laptop to face the front of the store, figuring it was either a college student or a harried mother looking for Pokemon or Magic the Gathering cards. Those types, beyond my regulars, are about all that trickle into my store on weekdays.

The man who came in was no college student, and he definitely wasn't a soccer mom. He walked through the door and paused, his head turning and his eyes wide from the change between daylight and the strategically placed lamps I keep in my shop. He took in the front display of the latest adventure releases and the wall rack of new-release comics, then stepped further in, head turning as though searching for something or someone.

His uncertainty gave me a moment to look him over. He looked roughly thirty years old and somewhat like a Hollywood version of a Norse God. About six foot six with shaggy white-blond hair, features that a romance novel would call chiseled, and more lean muscle than a CrossFit junkie. He was also packing a handgun, mostly hidden beneath his custom-fitted leather jacket.

So, you know, not your average comic book or tabletop gaming enthusiast.

There was also the part where my wards hummed for moment, a sound only I could hear. Which meant he wasn't human, either.

Not that this was weird for the town of Wylde, Idaho. Most of the non-college-student population isn't wholly human. We're the shape-shifter capital of the West. Harper herself is a fox shifter; two of the other three in my game group are a wolverine and a coyote. Guy who owns the pawnshop next to me is a bona fide leprechaun, and the woman who runs the bakery on the other side is some kind of witch or maybe a druid. The thick ley lines that run through the River of No Return Wilderness at the edge of town draw all kinds of supernaturals to the area.

It was what had drawn me here. I'd always heard the best place to hide a leaf is in a forest.

I was immediately on my guard. Wards aren't really my strong suit, so I didn't know what flavor of preternatural this giant was, but the gun didn't bode well. Nor did the way he looked at me like he recognized me, or the way he came over to the counter, moving with preternatural grace around the comic book displays. I gathered my power inside myself, preparing to send a bolt of pure energy into his chest if needed. I hadn't cast a real spell like that in years, but I figured I could get a single one off without knocking myself unconscious with the effort. Probably.

"Can I help you?" I asked, glad the counter was between us, even if the glass case full of dice and card boxes would be little more than a stutter step to clear for a shifter.

"Who are you?" he said. His voice was deep, with a slight accent. Russian maybe. His eyes were the blue of glacier ice and his expression about as welcoming.

"Jade Crow," I said, teeth grinding with the effort of speaking and keeping control of my magic. "Who are you?"

"Hi handsome," Harper said, climbing out of the overstuffed chair next to me that she'd been gaming in. She snapped her laptop shut and gave the newcomer a dazzling smile. She was angular and punky, with spiky brown hair and a way of making men forget what they were going to say when she smiled.

Then she stopped smiling and her eyes got huge, focusing in on the silver feather strung around his neck. "Oh, shit. Justice. Forgive me." And she bowed her head like she was addressing some kind of royalty.

"Justice? Like one of the shifter peacekeepers, right?" I said, my voice shaking a little with the effort of holding on to my powers for this long without letting loose. "The fuck is going on?" I glanced at Harper and then back at the intruder, keeping my eyes on the feather talisman. Yeah, it was better to look at his neck. Or his chin. His lips were way too kissable.

I shoved that thought away for later. Much, much later.

"I am Aleksei Kirov, a Justice of the Council of Nine. And you," he said, gesturing at me, "are a murderer."

"What?" Harper and I said at the same time. We shared a baffled glance. I hadn't killed anyone in my life, though not for lack of trying once. But still.

Behind the Justice, and invisible at the moment to anyone but myself, my spirit wolf guardian stirred, rising from where she'd been sleeping. Wolf didn't growl though, just cocked her head and stared at Aleksei, ready for trouble but clearly not expecting it quite yet.

"I haven't killed anyone. Ever." I let go of the magic inside me before I accidentally lost control and unleashed. Wiping the sweat from my forehead, I ran my shaky hands over my hair, and tugged my waist-length ponytail over my shoulder.

Aleksei relaxed as a confused look came over his face. "You tell the truth," he said. "But I saw you in a vision. The Nine sent me here. There are shifters in danger and you were at the center, at the crossroads between their lives and their deaths."

I opened my mouth. Closed it. A small chill went through me. The only way I could see shifters dying because of me was if *he* had found me. My psycho ex-mentor and lover. I started to mentally pray to the powers of the universe that *that* hadn't happened or we were all in deep, deep shit.

"Nobody is in danger that we know of," Harper said. "Uh, Justice," she added, still trying to look respectful.

What I knew of the Council of Nine was practically legend, the shifter version of gods. They had Justices, powerful shifters appointed to keep the peace among shifter populations, and to keep the secret of shifter existence from most of the human world. They were judge, jury, and executioner all in one. Shifters didn't get up to much crime, but if they did, the sentence was almost always death. Pretty good deterrent, I suppose.

"Besides, I'm not a shifter," I pointed out. "So you have no power over me."

"Unless you pose a danger to shifters. What are you?" Aleksei asked, his ice-chip eyes narrowing. Subtlety was apparently not one of his charms.

"She's a hedge witch," Harper answered for me. I was glad, since this Justice guy seemed to have the ability to detect lies. Harper wasn't lying because as far as she knew, that's what I was. She was just wrong.

Even though she was my best friend, I couldn't tell her the truth. I couldn't tell anyone that I was a sorceress. Because they'd all try to kill me, or at least drive me away. Nobody likes sorcerers. Probably because most of us are assholes who kill and eat the hearts of supernatural beings for their power.

I was saved from having to verbally confirm or deny my witchiness by Ciaran. He pushed through my front door, all four foot nothing of him, his copper and silver hair neatly combed and his red coat clinging to his plump body. I looked at the clock on my computer monitor and muttered a curse. It was later than I'd thought.

"Harper," Ciaran said with a nod and barely a glance at Aleksei. "Jade," he addressed me in Irish, "I'd really like you to come have that look at my things before I die of old age."

"For a man who watched Saint Pat drive out the snakes, you're looking fine to me," I said, also in Irish.

That leprechaun neighbor of mine I mentioned? That's Ciaran. He'd picked up a load of things in an auction the day before, and as always with old things he liked to have me check for magical auras and any hidden surprises. I didn't use my talents much out of fear of broadcasting my location, but minor magic like detection was as easy as breathing for me, so I did the neighborly thing and helped out when he needed.

"So, uh." I looked at Aleksei. "Since I haven't killed anyone and am not planning to, maybe you can just go Justice somewhere else? I'm closing shop."

"I will stay here. We will talk after. My visions are never wrong."

From how rigid he was and how intently he stared at me, I wondered if maybe he had a sword up his ass or something. "Okay, buddy. Just tone down the creepy before I get back. And you'll wait outside my store. I don't do strangers." Whoops. That came out weird. "In my store. I mean, alone. I mean I can't leave you here alone. So wait outside." Great. Now I was babbling.

"Fine," he said and I swear to the Universe the bastard smirked at me.

Ciaran's shop is an antiquer's paradise and a neat freak's nightmare. Also probably a nightmare if you have allergies. He kept it tidy, in its own cluttered way, but trying to keep dust off a few hundred old books, paintings, and curio cabinets full of knives, glassware, art plates, figurines, tools with unknown purpose, guns that last saw use during the Civil War, and other interesting items was a task even an immortal couldn't manage.

The shop had an almost smoky, magical feel that I loved. Above us, chandeliers of all kinds, from elk antlers to Waterford crystal, lit the place, casting shadows into the shadows until you felt as though you might come around a table piled with swords and find the wardrobe that leads to Narnia. The air wasn't musty; it was perfumed with orange and clove and some sort of citrus sent from whatever Ciaran used to wipe down the tables. The best part was that sometimes Ciaran really did have a magical item or two, though it was rare and he generally had me destroy them if we couldn't figure out what they did. Letting normals buy magical things was just asking for later trouble that nobody wanted.

"Hey," I whispered to Harper as we entered the shop, "what flavor is that Justice, anyway?"

"Flavor?" she whispered back. "Scary with a dollop of sexy?"

"No, like animal flavor," I said, whacking the back of her head with my palm.

"Oh. Tiger." She grinned and rubbed her head.

"Figures," I muttered. "Guess he wouldn't be, like, a rabbit or something." I'd bet a week of earnings he would be the biggest damn tiger ever. Shifter animals were usually larger than real-world ones anyway, but odds were that cocky bastard would be like the strongest, prettiest tiger ever to live. The universe was just like that.

"Most shifters are predators," Harper said, ducking in front of me. "Makes sense someone who has to hunt bad shifters and stuff would be a super predator, right?"

"You two done gossiping?" Ciaran called back to us. He was already halfway through the store.

Harper and I wound our way through the tables and cabinets toward the back office where Ciaran kept any interesting purchases for me to go over, just in case, before putting them out on the floor.

"Was at an auction in Seattle last month," Ciaran explained, using English for Harper's benefit. "Just got the goods shipped in today. Some old pieces; might be worth checking out before I put a price on them. Even found some of those silver buttons your mum likes so much, Azalea."

Harper wrinkled her nose at him. He knew she hated being called by her name and preferred her gamer handle. She was about to reply when she stopped cold in front of me, forcing me to do a little dance sideways to avoid running into her. My arm whacked a cabinet and it jingled and rocked but settled without breaking anything. Thank the universe. I figure if something ever fell in here, it would domino and the whole place would crash like a bad YouTube video.

"Where… how… no… I…" Harper couldn't get words out. She just pointed at a large stuffed fox that was perched on top of an oriental dresser.

"What about it, love? Are you all right?" Ciaran reached for Harper as she started to sink to the floor with horrible half-mewing, half-gulping cries.

I caught her first, wrapping my arms around her wiry body and finally seeing her face. Tears made her mascara run, and her shoulders shook in my arms.

"That's Rosie," she gasped. "That's my mom!"

Through the power of Irish hospitality or maybe some magical leprechaun mojo, Ciaran had Harper bundled in a sweater and holding a cup of mint tea before she even realized she'd finally stopped sobbing. Which was good, because Aleksei, who insisted Harper now call him Alek instead of Justice, was grilling her and Ciaran like a cop pushing a suspect.

To be fair, I don't think he intended it to come out that way. I'd known him for maybe half an hour now and it seemed he only had one gear and it was stuck on one level: intense.

"I will go through my records, Jade, and see if I can get the ID of the man that sold this to me, all right?"

Ciaran said. "It was a young man, on Tuesday, I remember that much."

"See it done." Alek turned his icy glare on Harper. His gaze seemed to soften, but it was hard to tell. "And why did no one notice her missing all this time? You said she's been gone since last weekend."

"Because she was out picking mushrooms," I said, stepping firmly between Alek and Harper. "Rose does that. She'll be gone in those woods a week or so. It's normal for her."

"How would a poacher get her?" Harper choked out. "She shouldn't have even been in fox form."

She was right about that. Rose, her mother, ran a bed and breakfast on a ranch that was grandfathered into the River of No Return Wilderness. She was an earthy, eccentric, and loving woman who took all sorts of shifter strays in. She liked to go camping in the wilderness every spring before the summer season brought in wildlife photographers, whitewater rafters, hikers, and all the other people the Wilderness Area attracted.

"I was sent here by the Council," Alek said and he shook his head, eyes narrowing speculatively at me. "That means foul play."

"Hey, I was manning my shop. Plus I wouldn't touch a gun even if it snuggled and made me waffles." I glared at him. "Oh, Universe damn you. Now you are interrogating me. This is not cool."

"My vision says you are the key," he said, folding impressively muscled arms over his broad chest.

"Maybe you need your psychic eyes checked," I shot back.

"Guys," Harper said, sniffling. "Please. We need to find out how Mom… oh God, I can't say it. Just. Help me."

I turned to her, taking the tea from her hands and setting it aside. She collapsed into my arms, shaking with renewed sobs. I couldn't resist another glare at Alek, making it clear this was definitely his fault.

"Hey! Jade? Ciaran?" a male voice called out from back within the shop.

Fuck. Game night.

"Ezee, Levi, we're back here," I yelled to them, then said to Alek as his hand reached for his gun, "Ease off there, Dirty Harry. They're furry friendlies."

"Is anyone human in this town?" he asked. He'd already sniffed at Ciaran and established he was safe, since he wasn't a normal.

"Steve," Harper said, swallowing another sob and wiping her nose on the now damp sleeve of Ciaran's sweater.

"Harper? You okay? What's going on?" The twins had made their way back to us.

Ezekiel and Levi Chapowits are Native American like myself, but Nez Perce, not Crow. They're fraternal, not identical twins, but they share a lot of the same features. Strong bone structure, above average height, thick black hair, dark eyes. Beyond that, and being giant nerds, they are nothing alike. Ezee is a coyote shifter and wears designer knockoff suits he sews himself. He teaches American History and Native Studies up at Juniper College.

Levi is a wolverine who wears nothing but cargo pants, work boots, and tee-shirts stained with the guts of the cars he works on in his shop. He wears his hair in a long Mohawk and has enough piercings in his face that I joke I could peel his skin and use it to strain pasta.

They both break the heart of every woman they meet, pretty much. Not just because they are handsome, smart, and awesome, but because Levi is happily married to a crazy hippie artist and owl shifter named Junebug and Ezee is as gay as Neil Patrick Harris.

"Someone killed Mom," Harper blurted out.

"Frakking-A," Ezee said. "That why there's a Justice here?"

Trust Ezee to have noticed the tall, hot guy and taken in the feather talisman in a glance.

"What?" Levi said. "Oh, hello." He tipped his head to Alek.

Alek nodded back, finally seeming at a loss for words in the face of the twins. I was certain he'd start interrogating them soon enough, however.

"Where's Rose? What happened?" Levi asked.

"Behind you," I said softly.

A lot more curse words came from the twins as they looked Rose's dead body over.

"I don't see a wound," Ezee said finally.

"We should get an autopsy. That's what they do on TV." Harper pulled the sweater tight around herself and stood up.

"Is your medical examiner shifter also?" Alek asked.

"No," Levi said. "He's with County. We aren't big enough to have our own." Levi also was a volunteer firefighter. That kind of multitasking happens when you live as long as shifters do and in a small town like Wylde.

I ran my hands over Rose's body, swallowing bile as nausea wormed through me. I was manhandling one of my favorite people in the world. My eyes felt too tight and hot in their sockets and I realized I was about to cry. Shit. I never cry. Not in a couple decades. Not anymore.

I don't know much about taxidermy, but I figured there would be seams, staples, something. I felt nothing but her fur, its longer russet hairs rough and the lighter undercoat thick and soft on my fingers. I looked into her creepily realistic glass eyes and wished I could ask her what the hell she'd been doing in fox form and how she'd gotten caught. It was possible whoever had done this had no idea he'd killed and stuffed a person.

Which didn't make my desire to hunt him down and stuff him any less rage-filled and immediate.

"Vivian Lake can do it," I said. "She's the local vet. Wolf shifter," I added, seeing the look on Alek's face. I took a deep breath as I stepped away from Rose.

Time to put on my Game Master face and get shit done.

"Levi, call Steve. Tell him no game tonight, family emergency. Ezee, you take Harper up to my place." I pulled out my keys and tossed them to him. Harper looked as though she'd protest for a moment but then leaned into Ezee with another sob.

"Thank you, Jade," she whispered. "I don't think I can, I mean…" she trailed off.

"I know. It's okay. We'll figure this out. You have a car?" I said, turning back to Alek.

Ciaran came down the back stairs from his own apartment with a blanket, holding it out. I gave him a half-smile of thanks, glad he'd foreseen that we would want something to carry her in.

Before I could, Alek took the blanket and wrapped Rose up with a gentle carefulness that surprised me. As presumptuous as he was, I was kind of glad I didn't have to touch her again. He looked at me, apparently waiting for me to lead the way out. Another surprise. Maybe he wasn't always a macho asshole. Or maybe he just wanted to keep me in front of him so he could keep an eye on me. I shoved away those thoughts.

"Okay, Justice, since I'm betting you'll want to be there, let's go see Dr. Lake."

Alek didn't let me drive his truck. Guess the surprises had run out. It wasn't what Harper and I would joke was a "compensating for it" truck, but a good-sized Ford with scratches and dents and a little dirt around the edges that let you know this guy used his truck for things, not just for driving around. The interior smelled of wet grass, damp earth, and a vanilla-laced musk that I was pretty sure came from Alek himself.

My whole body, all my senses, was aware of the huge, handsome man only inches away from me. Not a thing that boded well. The last time I'd been this instantly attracted to someone, he'd tried to fatten me up with magic, Hansel and Gretel style, and then eat my heart. I inched my ass as close to the door as possible, putting a bit more gap between us on the bench seat.

The drive to Dr. Lake's should have taken about five minutes, but we hit the single stop light on Main and it was red. An old woman, someone I didn't recognize—which meant she was not a nerd and probably part of the human half of Wylde—inched her way across the crosswalk.

"Where are you staying?" I asked, more out of a need to fill the silence and not think about what was inside the hand-sewn quilt on my lap. There were two tiny motels in town, mostly catering to the college for visiting family, and the summer tourists.

"I have a house trailer," he said. "It's at the Mikhail and Sons RV Park, you know it?"

Of course I knew it. Mikhail and his two sons were bear shifters. Vasili, the younger son, had a thing for Magic the Gathering cards. His purchases paid my building rent every time a new expansion came out. They were good people. I could just imagine how they'd bent over backward to accommodate a Justice. I bet they hadn't charged him. I wasn't going to ask that aloud. I was more curious about this whole vision thing of his.

"So how's that Justice thing work? Do you just get visions and know where to show up? And why didn't you see Rose in danger?" I hadn't meant that last part to sound so accusatory, but fuck it. What's the point of a supernatural system of law if they can't help people before someone gets killed?

"Is like a compass," he said, turning his head to look at me. His eyes were no longer ice chips but deep pools, and there was something sad in his gaze. "I know where to go; I know that I will be needed. The visions are what the Nine know, what they share with me in my dreams. I only know what they know. Is not my power, but theirs."

I noticed his accent got stronger, and wondered if I'd upset him. It was hard to tell since his chiseled face gave away little.

"From what Harper has told me, the Nine are like gods. Can't they do a little better than vague visions?"

"They are not gods," Alek said. "And there is much in the world we cannot control." His tone and the sudden tightness in his jaw and shoulders warned me this was a dangerous subject.

"Hey, green light," I said, too brightly. The car behind us, clearly someone important and in a hurry, honked.

We rode the last couple minutes in silence. I wanted to ask him more about the vision of me, about me being somehow the crossroads between people living and dying. He seemed to think that meant I was killing people, but the most likely explanation was a lot scarier than that. If Samir, my ex, had found me, everyone I knew was in danger. Maybe his vision had nothing to do with whoever had killed Rose.

I took a deep breath and hugged the bundle, my eyes hot again with unshed tears.

"Left, into that parking lot," I said, pointing to Dr. Lake's practice. It was in a Victorian-style house—like a lot of us business owners in Wylde, Dr. Lake lived on the floor above her practice.

Alek came around and opened my door, taking Rose from me. I led the way into the office. Christie, a young wolf shifter who does reception for Dr. Lake, was the only one inside and I sighed with relief.

"Hey Christie, the doc in?" I asked.

"Yeah, she's doing paperwork," Christie said, eyeing the large bundle Alek carried. Or perhaps she was just eyeing Alek.

"Get her, and tell her we'll be in the surgery room. Then you might want to close early. Just trust me, okay?" I really didn't want to show the body to Christie. She was barely out of her teens.

"Uh, okay." She didn't like it, but she got up and ran down the hall to Dr. Lake's office.

I led the way to the surgery room. The smell of alcohol tinged with an undertone of old blood make my skin goosebump. I knew the vet pretty well, since Harper was always rescuing hurt animals a sideswipe away from roadkill and begging me to take them to the vet for her. She couldn't stomach the times there was nothing to be done but easing the little critters into death, so I got the fun task of hearing Dr. Lake say there was nothing to do but help them cross over.

Dr. Lake came in directly after us. She was a tiny wolf shifter, short enough she would have legally needed a booster seat in the state of California, with a wiry, compact energy about her. She halted and tipped her chin up, her nostrils flaring as she sniffed the air. If I didn't hang out with shifters practically twenty-four-seven, it would have been creepy, but you get used to shifters sniffing people to recognize them or learn their mood or whatever.

"Another of Harper's creatures?" she asked.

"Not exactly," I said. I took the bundle from Alek and set Rose on the stainless steel table, unfolding the blanket.

"That animal is dead," Dr. Lake said. "And has been stuffed. There's nothing I can do here."

"It's Rose Macnulty," I said softly. "We need to figure out how she died."

Dr. Lake's eyes widened and she took a half-step back, looking from Rose to me and finally to Alek. "Ah, Justice. This is a Council issue?"

"Shifter getting murdered is always a Council issue."

"Can you do an autopsy?" I asked. It wasn't really a question, since I bet she'd do whatever the big old Justice here told her to do, but no reason to ruffle more fur than Alek already was just by being himself.

Dr. Lake stepped up to the table and ran her hands expertly over Rose's body. She peeled back the fox's lips, felt along her belly, examined her paws. With a grunt she nodded.

"I have no idea how they did it, but I'll open her and see if I can find out from the inside. No seams, no bullet wounds. It's an expert job." She shook her head. "Let me glove up. Get her on the table proper; no point getting that quilt icky."

I lifted Rose up so Alek could pull the blanket out. Nausea swept through me again, along with an electric tingle along my skin.

And I knew, with lightning clarity, where I'd felt that before.

It wasn't just revulsion at the body, I was touching foreign magic. There are lots of kinds of magic and lots of ways to draw power. I drew my power from myself, from something like a well inside of myself. It's unique to me. Any other kind of power—be it from a witch's ritual drawing on ley lines or natural forces, or another sorcerer—feels alien and weird to me. I can't use it or understand it, only sense it. Like being a native English speaker and finding all the books in your house suddenly written in Chinese. You know it says something, but the hell if you could tell anyone what that was.

"Wait," I said. I closed my eyes, reaching for a thread of my own power. I gritted my teeth and ran my hands along Rose's side. The wrongness resolved into a more solid impression. Black lines, dark on dark behind my eyelids, wrapped all around her body just beneath the skin before terminating in a complex knot in her chest.

And below that, the faint *bump-bump* of a heartbeat.

"Shit," I said, stumbling backward. "Don't cut. She's not dead. She's got a heartbeat."

"What?" Alek and Dr. Lake asked at the same time.

"It's magic. She's not dead. She's frozen somehow. Like stasis." I shivered. Dead might have been better. I couldn't imagine being frozen, unable to move or speak. Cut off from my human form.

"Can you do something about it?" Alek asked me. I didn't like the speculative way he was looking at me.

"No," I said. The truth, more or less. "This is way above my pay grade," which was kind of a lie, but I hoped not enough of one that his apparent lie-detection abilities would notice. "It's not a kind of magic I can use. Whoever cast the spell has to undo it. If that's even possible." All that was the truth. Great universe, I hoped it was possible. If it wasn't, Rose would be trapped like this until the spell degraded enough to stop keeping her alive—and that could be years or even centuries, depending on how exactly this magic worked.

"So I find who did this and make them undo it before I kill them. Good." Alek turned toward the door.

"Hold up there, Rambo. I need a ride back to my store." Not that I was looking forward to telling Harper what we'd found. I didn't know if not-quite-dead was worse. We had no answers, just more questions.

"I will keep Rose here, if you want, and see if I can figure out a way to monitor her vitals," Dr. Lake said, talking to Alek as much as to me. "If anything changes, I'll call you, Jade."

The light stayed green on the way back through town and this time we didn't talk at all.

Ezee, Levi, and Harper were waiting for us in my apartment over the store. I led Alek up the back steps. Three red-eyed faces greeted us as we came into my small living room. The apartment is a long, narrow one-bedroom unit, with a single bathroom. The living area is dominated by my purple velvet couch and a fifty-five-inch LED TV with about every console you can name set up under it. I mostly use my Xbox360, but some days nothing will do but to kill my thumbs playing Armada on my Sega Dreamcast.

A girl needs options. To me, video games are like shoes. But with more pixels and a plot.

Ezee and Levi had Harper, still bundled in Ciaran's red sweater, between them. As we came in, they each took one of her hands and turned their faces to us, expectant.

"So," I said with a weak smile. "You want the good news or the bad news?"

"Mom's dead. There is no good news. Unless on the way to the vet you ran over the guy responsible." Harper glared at me, her green eyes puffy and glittering with tears.

"Actually, she isn't dead. That's the good news. And kind of the bad news, too." I grimaced. That hadn't come out in the sympathetic, gentle way I'd rehearsed in my head.

"She's not dead? But I saw her. She was… how?" I could almost see the hope like will-o-the-wisp lights turning on in Harper's eyes. I just prayed it wasn't a false hope I was giving her. How much worse would this get if Alek couldn't find the magic user who did this and make him or her undo it?

"Magic," I said. "She's under some kind of spell holding her in her animal form and keeping her frozen like that."

"Why the hell would someone do that?" Levi said.

"Good fucking question." I shook my head and looked at Alek. He had come to loom beside me, standing too damn close for my comfort, but I wasn't about to inch away. It would have looked pretty obvious.

"I will ask when I find him," Alek said with a tiny smile that made me think about screaming rabbits and blood spraying on white walls. Not a nice smile, really.

"I don't care why," Harper yelled. "Just find him and make him undo it."

Ciaran knocked at the back door before entering the tense, now-quiet room. He was out of breath and excited. "I have the paperwork. Here." He held out a manila folder.

I took it and spread it open on the narrow black coffee table after clearing away the remotes and controllers. The photocopy of the ID said the guy who sold Rose was named Caleb Greer, age thirty-two, with an address in Boise, Idaho. Brown hair, brown eyes, five-foot-eight, one hundred and fifty pounds.

"He was thinner than that photo. If his ID hadn't put him at over thirty, I would have thought he was a college student," Ciaran said.

"He probably is," Ezee said. He leaned forward, looking at the paperwork upside-down. "I mean, how likely is it that some middle-aged dude from Boise drove all the way out here to sell a stuffed fox? It's more likely a fake or stolen ID."

"I have his signature on the sale, and his fingerprints, there, see? I do everything above board," Ciaran said. He folded his arms and pressed his lips into a line, muttering in Irish about idiot dogs.

"So, what, we just go start knocking on dorm room doors until Ciaran recognizes someone?" Levi asked.

"If that's what it takes," Harper said. The hope in her eyes had turned into anger.

I resisted making a comment about anger leading to hate and hate leading to the dark side, but the tension and level of predatory desire to kill was pretty palpable in the room. While it made a lot of sense in a "someone did something awful to someone I love" way, unleashing the hounds, so to speak, on the mostly normals population of Juniper College seemed like a pretty bad plan in actuality. For all we knew, some kid had found the be-spelled Rose on the side of the road with a "free" sign on her and figured they could score a little extra cash.

"There's a better way," I said, mentally kicking myself even as my mouth kept moving. I shouldn't do magic. I shouldn't get involved. I felt like Sarah in *Labyrinth* when she falls down into the chute full of hands and chooses to keep going down. Too late now.

"I can do a spell," I continued. "There's enough with the signature and fingerprint that I can probably design a tracking thingy. If he or she is within twenty miles, it'll point right at them." There, that was more or less the truth. I carefully didn't look at Alek, though I could feel him looking intently at me. He didn't trust me anyway, so fuck him.

Hmm. Fucking Alek.

My brain hung up on that idea for a moment and I had to ask Harper to repeat herself once I realized she'd asked me something.

"What do you need?"

Technically, I didn't need anything. But I wasn't about to go along. This was clearly Justice business. If the kid was involved, nothing I could do would stop the death sentence on his head for messing with shifters. Justices were judge, jury, and executioners. In most of the world outside the shifter-dense population of Wylde, shifters hid, maintaining a careful line between themselves and normals. Anyone stepping over the line risked humans finding out about the things that go bump in the night on a larger scale, and nobody wanted that. The Inquisition? The Nazis? Not just about persecuting humans. A lot of shifters, warlocks, and witches had gotten caught up in human madness over the centuries.

The Council of Nine and the system of Justices keeping peace and shifter law had come about sometime after the worst of the Inquisition, from what Ezee had told me. Compared to outright slaughter and experimentation, the inflexibility of shifter law was pretty understandable.

"A compass," I said. "I have the rest of what I need here."

"I will be right back," Ciaran said, turning and dashing back out my door.

He came back with a brass compass done up to look like an old-fashioned pocket watch.

"Perfect. Just give me a minute." I took the compass and the folder and went into my bedroom, locking the door behind me.

Deep breath. This wouldn't take a lot of magic. We'd still be safe. Wylde has so many ley lines, a full coven of witches, a couple thousand shifters, and probably a few other paranormals I didn't yet know about. One tiny spell wouldn't give me away. Probably.

Wolf materialized from thin air, like she does, and jumped up on my bed, watching me with her head cocked and ears perked. I couldn't tell if she approved or not.

I sank down onto my knees and put the compass on the floor on top of the thumbprint. Wrapping one hand around the large silver polyhedral die that hangs around my neck, I focused, bringing my magic up from the deep well inside.

This kind of magic isn't my specialty. In my old life, before I almost got killed and eaten, I was more of a fireball throwing, showy sorceress. Form a magic sword instantly out of ice that won't melt? No problem. Want to cause a localized earthquake or rain down acid? Again, I could do that, once upon a time. Samir and I used to train in an abandoned bunch of warehouses he'd bought up in Detroit, sometimes going out to lone islands in the Great Lakes to do the really spectacular stuff.

I'd grown up and honed my magic on Dungeons & Dragons manuals in the nineteen eighties, raised by an awesome bunch of programmers and gamers after my family kicked me out. Todd, Kayla, Sophie, and Ji-hoon had taken me in after I'd spent a hellish year on the streets of New York. They had been the closest thing to real family I'd ever had after my birth family kicked me out. Until Samir destroyed that, too.

Another deep breath. I let the past flow away from me and focused on the fingerprint, its ridges and whorls etched in black ink. There wasn't really a DnD spell precedent for what I wanted to do, but that was okay. Role playing games are just that, games. They aren't any more real than Godzilla or He-Man. I'd used the spells as a sort of channel when I was growing up, a way of learning how to focus and impose my will on the power that flowed naturally within me.

I focused on the fingerprint, then on the idea of the hand that had formed the signature. My power flared into my amulet and poured down into the compass. The needle twitched, then spun, then stopped, pointing not north but now to the northwest. Toward Juniper College.

I sealed the spell with another focusing of my will, visualizing a thread of power like a monofilament line from the d-twenty around my neck to the compass. It would hold until I let it go or it got too far away, keeping the compass connected to my power.

"Wish that kid luck," I muttered to Wolf as I rose and took the compass back out into the living room.

"Here." I handed the compass to Alek. "This will point you right to the owner of that fingerprint. And, uh, be careful. Whoever did that to Rose isn't a nice person."

"I am not a nice person," Alek said with another killer-inside-me smile. "And I have certain defenses from magic that most do not have."

I almost asked but managed to close my mouth before it got him even more suspicious of me.

"Find him and make him undo the spell. Promise me, Justice." Harper's hands were curled into white fists in her lap as she spat the words out. I couldn't actually tell if she'd asked him to promise her justice or if she was using his title. Maybe both.

Alek started to shake his head as he said "I will..." but I pinched the back of his thigh and twisted, hard, giving him my best don't-you-dare-crush-my-friend look.

"I will do my best," he amended, with only a slight twitch of a smile in reaction. Maybe he didn't completely hate me. Great.

He had really firm thighs. I shoved that thought away into the overflowing paper bag in my head labeled "inappropriate thoughts about Alek."

After he left, another awkward silence descended. Harper finally broke it by standing up. "Where's Mom?"

"With Dr. Lake," I said. "She wanted to keep her under observation, monitor her vitals. She'll call me if there is any change." I tapped my jean's pocket where my phone was jammed. Under observation and monitoring vitals sounded good, clinical and nice, like Rose was just in the hospital after an accident instead of locked magically into her fox body, paralyzed and helpless.

Okay. My thoughts really weren't on the helpful train today.

"I want to go home," Harper said. "But I don't know if I can face Max. Oh God." At the thought of her brother, her eyes started leaking again.

"We'll go with you," Levi said.

"Yeah, of course," Ezee and I agreed.

"Okay. But maybe we don't say anything. I don't know. I need to think." Harper took a deep breath and stood up.

"I'll be at my place, if you need me," Ciaran said, excusing himself.

"Thank you, Ciaran," I said, squeezing his arm as we all moved toward the door. "And Harper, we'll say or not say whatever you want. It's going to be okay."

I could have stabbed myself for saying that last part, but the look of hope she gave me made the lie worth it. Hell, for all I knew, maybe it wasn't a lie. Maybe the Justice was as badass as he thought and he'd kick in a door or drag the guy who did this back to Dr. Lake's, and we'd be having tea and cookies with Rose in her country-chic kitchen by moonrise.

After all, in a world full of shape shifters, witches, gods, and sorcerers, maybe miracles can happen.

Dusk fell over us like a shroud as we drove out of the town proper and down the narrow two-lane road toward The Henhouse Bed and Breakfast which Harper and her family called home. I rode in the back of Levi's Honda Civic with Harper but we all drove in silence, each lost in our own thoughts, I guess.

The locals, like my friends in the car, call the River of No Return Wilderness "the Frank," after the prefix, since it's technically the Frank Church River of No Return Wilderness. I resisted calling it that, but in bleak moments like this its name fit. No return. Whatever happened after tonight, after finding Rose and whatever dark magic was trapping her like that, nothing would be exactly the same here. We were friends, sure, but we'd never faced any real adversity together. We sat around a table a couple times a week and pretended we were mages and bards and barbarians fighting dragons and evil lich kings.

I stared out the window so that I wouldn't be staring creepily at Harper and watched as the sun disappeared in a bloody smear behind the black spikes of the fir and pine trees.

Yeah. My brain wasn't feeling morbid and hopeless at all.

"Do you think she's awake? Conscious, I mean. Like, could she hear me?" Harper said softly. Her face was still pressed to the window, her eyes staring out into the darkening trees.

I knew what she meant. I'd been worrying over the same questions. I had no real answer, though. Harper had asked me what I thought, so I decided that would allow another small lie. It's almost funny how we destroy things by inches.

"I think she's sleeping. Magic like that takes a ritual. I bet she was asleep and still is. Big, blond, and scary out there will find the bastard that did it and stop him. Then she'll wake up, like Sleeping Beauty." I smiled at her in what I hoped was a reassuring way.

"But without the rape and having a baby after one hundred years thing," Ezee said over the back of his seat.

"Oh God, what if he did things to her before the spell? Or after?" Harper started sobbing again.

"Not helping, dumbass." I leaned in and flicked Ezee's ear.

"Alek will find him," Levi said. "The Nine never fail to get some kind of justice."

"We should have gone with him," Harper said. "I should have."

"And what?" I said. "None of us have law enforcement backgrounds. None of us know shit about tracking down someone or how to deal with hostile magic." Wow, I was just full of lies tonight. Why quit when you're ahead, right? "We'd be in the way. Remember what you guys told me about the Justices? They are highly trained from, like, birth, and equipped to act as supernatural judge, jury, and executioner. I don't think any of us want to get in the way of that."

"I guess," Harper said, sitting up a little.

"We could always nerd the guy to death, I suppose," Levi said.

"Ooh, yeah, new torture technique. We'll make him watch nothing but *Highlander II* and *Star Trek V*!" Ezee twisted in his seat, reaching back to squeeze Harper's knee.

Harper giggled a little through her hiccupping sobs. "Anyone would give up their secrets to make that stop, huh?" Her smile was pretty weak-sauce, but at least she wasn't staring blankly out the window and letting her mind run all kinds of horror scenarios.

My phone started playing the Mega Man 2 theme, and I fumbled it out of my pocket. Ciaran.

"'Sup?"

"Two men, guns," Ciaran said quickly in Irish. In the background I heard someone, a male voice for sure, say something about speaking English and Ciaran say it was just a greeting. Then he continued, and it sounded from the echo like he had me on speakerphone. "Jade, there's a problem with that stuffed fox I sold you. Sorry about the late hour, but could you bring it by the shop as soon as possible?"

"Sure thing. I've got it with me. I can be there in thirty?" It would only take us maybe fifteen to get back into town if Levi stepped on it.

"Sounds good. Come in the front, I'll leave it open for you."

"Cool. See you soon."

I made sure the phone call was disconnexted and then growled at Levi. "Turn the car around. Two men with guns have Ciaran and are looking for Rose. We have to go back."

Levi hit the brakes and executed the quickest three-point turn I ever want to experience ever, or make that *never*, again. His car might look compact and reliable, but inside is a beast of an engine that probably isn't even street legal and we felt the full g-forces of it as he floored the gas and shot us back toward town.

"Call the sheriff?" Ezee asked.

"Not yet. We don't know what we're dealing with and I don't want to get Ciaran killed. Let me go in and see. If I'm not out in a few, you guys can call then. I'll leave my phone line open to you so you can hear."

"How come you get to go in?" Harper said. "If they want my mom, they'll have to go through me. I don't fear bullets." She looked ready to go furry and get her serial killer on.

"They are expecting me. Going psycho on them might feel good, but it won't really solve anything. Also, we don't know yet what we are dealing with. They might be human, in which case killing them is kind of murder and even our cops might get mad about it," I said. The local sheriff was an elected position, so of course she was a shifter, but I think the last time our town saw an actual murder was back in the era of buggies and gunslingers in saloons wearing ten gallon hats.

"Can you go faster?" Harper said.

"Maybe," Levi answered.

He could, it turns out. We got to Ciaran's store in less than fifteen minutes, slowing down to drive past it and not look like maniacs. The main street was almost abandoned after dark in our sleepy little down. Most people would be at the bars on the other end or over at the diner. All the shops were closed here and there was no foot traffic.

We pulled an emergency blanket out of the back of the Honda and I shook it out and then crumpled it into a bundle in my arms. They were expecting someone to bring something in, after all. I figured worst case I could use the blanket as a lame distraction.

"Okay. Harper, stay out here by the car and keep an eye on the front." She started to protest and I gave her my best pleading look. "Trust me? I need you out here watching my back."

When she finally nodded and her shoulders slumped, I continued with my plan. "Levi and Ezee, head around back. If I'm not out in ten or if I say anything about my grandmother over the phone, call Sheriff Lee. I don't suppose anyone thought to get Alek's number?" I sure hadn't. I touched my amulet. The spell was still active, the link thick and strong. Alek likely wasn't far away if he still had the compass.

Head shakes met that last question. "Okay. It doesn't matter. Don't get shot."

Easy for me to say, I thought as I walked into Ciaran's Curios. The store was dark except for a light in the back hallway from the open office door. The dimness only emphasized the odd shadows cast by various lamps, statues, cabinets, and other items. I'd never noticed this place was so creepy at night.

I'd never walked in here expecting armed men, either. Correlation is not causation, but I could make a pretty good case on this one.

I tried to quiet my random thoughts and come up with a real plan other than *don't get shot.* I thought about using magic to somehow subdue the men, but just upkeeping the tracking spell was making me more tired than I thought it would. A headache had viselike fingers around my temples.

Magic for a sorcerer is like a muscle; if you don't use it much, you won't completely lose it, but it will atrophy and not work the same later. I did exercise my power on weekends sometimes, lifting small rocks and holding them up in various patterns. Nothing big, nothing that would jiggle Samir's web of informants or sensors or however he tracked me, and bring him after me like a starving spider.

Maybe I could do something more coincidental, like more White Wolf mage than Dungeons & Dragons mage. Jam the guns. Knock a cabinet onto their heads.

Only, I had no idea how to jam a gun. Nor did I have a clue how much magic would get me noticed. The ley lines and supernatural population could only hide so much, especially from someone who knew my magic and what it looked and felt like.

So, I was down to just winging it. No magic. Maybe I should have gone to my place first and grabbed a knife. I recalled some saying about bringing a knife to a gunfight and it not being a good thing. Okay, we were down to hoping I could take out two men with only my wits and a scratchy wool blanket. Great plan.

"Ciaran? I've got the fox," I called out as I carefully wove my way through the shop. I didn't want to surprise anyone with a gun.

"In my office," Ciaran called out.

I saw a shadow move in the hallway beyond the office. It was way too big to be the leprechaun. One of the gunmen?

Then I caught a gleam of eyes, the way a cat's eyes pick up light and shine in the dark. Alek stepped just enough forward that I could make out his features but he hung back so that he was still hidden from anyone inside the office itself. He raised a finger to his lips, and then made a *get away* motion. I shook my head.

"Ciaran," I called out again. "It's really dark out here. Can you come turn on a light or something? I feel like I'm going to kill myself running into something and this fox is super bulky."

There was muttering from the office. I crept forward, trying to be stealthy and not knock over anything. I let the blanket slide down my body to the floor and kicked it under a table, ready to follow it if bullets started flying.

"Be right there," Ciaran yelled.

He emerged from the office, a taller, thinner man standing directly behind him. I assumed that guy had the gun pointed at Ciaran's back.

"Drop the gun and tell your friend not to do anything stupid." Alek's voice was calm and deep. And cold enough to send chills down my spine.

"Fuck, man," said the guy behind Ciaran. He twisted his head and saw Alek's huge form in the shadows, pointing a big handgun at his head. "Jimmy, don't do anything stupid."

"There's a guy here with a gun," someone, I assumed Jimmy, said from inside the office. "What do we do? What? No, don't. Don't do that. We're sorry. We can fix this. Shit!"

The guy in the hallway turned slightly toward the door. "What's he doing?"

Ciaran chose that moment to sprint forward and then duck aside, behind a large oriental cabinet. Panicking, the guy with the gun started shooting into the dark shop as he swung around toward Alek.

I dove for the floor as well as something hot hit my hip. I felt as much as heard my phone shatter, and then lightning pain shot through my side and down my leg. I crawled with zero dignity under the table.

From my agonizing but safe-ish position, I saw Alek jumped by another man, this one shorter and bulkier than the first. They grappled and the first guy ran right at me, though I wasn't sure he could see me. In a brilliantly thought-out move, I shoved the wadded-up blanket next to me out in front of him and he sprawled into the table, knocking down the universe knows what around us.

The pain in my leg nearly blacked out my vision but I grabbed at the guy. He knew what had been done to Rose. He was the key; I couldn't let Harper down just because of a stupid wound.

"No. You. Don't," I hissed.

He stopped fighting me so suddenly I actually lost my grip. For a moment he froze and then he ripped at his neck, pulling out a medallion on a chain. I couldn't make out the details in the dim light but nausea hit me and I felt the same kind of weird magic that had trapped Rose at work.

"No no no nononono." The man's voice became a litany as the medallion started to glow a sickly green.

In pain, bleeding, and out of options, I reached for my power almost on instinct, throwing my power into a giant silver circle around us both, trying to lock out the foreign magic. Whatever that thing was doing, it didn't seem good.

The other gunman was screaming, and I dimly heard Alek cursing. Then it stopped, the sickly green light winking out as though I'd imagined it. The man in front of me lay still, his chest slowly rising and falling, but for all appearances he wasn't conscious.

"Jade!" Harper's voice.

Ciaran threw on the lights and I winced, blinking rapidly to try to adjust. Harper came up, kicking the gun further from the man's hand. Boy, really, now that I had a look at him. I doubted he was over twenty-one.

"It's a trap," I said, waving at Harper to back off. "Get an axe."

"Trick, not trap. Geez." She poked him with her shoe.

Misquoting *Army of Darkness*. I really was hurt. I crawled forward, trying to keep my weight off my injured hip. I felt the bullet inside me, my body reacting to the unknown object and trying to heal it out. I needed to get out of here before I did fully heal or there would be some truly uncomfortable questions.

But I wanted the boy's medallion. I yanked it off his neck as I pretended to feel for a pulse and slid it into my bra as I curled my body to keep the bleeding side out of Harper's vision.

I failed.

"Did you get shot? You're bleeding." Harper yanked off her teeshirt and bent over me, trying to press it to my hip.

"My phone broke when I dove under the table," I said, taking her shirt and covering the bloody patch as best I could. I didn't want to look yet. If it looked anything like it felt, my side was a disaster. "Just cuts. I'll be fine."

"We called Sheriff Lee, she's on her way," Ezee said. "Bloody hell, did you get shot?"

I had to get out there. Like, now.

"No, just cuts. I'm going to my place to clean up. This guy needs a medic or something. I don't know what happened." I tried to stand and regretted my life.

"This one is dead. I'm not sure how." Alek's voice.

Dead? Oh, that was bad. It was getting harder to think. I decided to worry about one thing at a time. Step one was figuring out how to walk out of here, up the stairs to my apartment, and if I could make it to the bathtub before I fainted from the pain. Be a lot easier to clean blood out of the bathroom than my living room carpet. I'd never get that security deposit back. Which was okay, since I owed it to myself, but still. I was a mean landlord.

"Harper, go with Jade. The less people messed up in this, the better, no?" Ciaran said.

"I've got to stay, since I called the sheriff," Levi said.

"And I do also, since she'll never believe only one of us was here," Ezee added.

"I've got her," Alek said. He moved with insane speed to my side and then somehow I was in his arms. "Don't protest," he whispered in Russian, his breath warm on my hair. "Clearly you don't want them to know you've been shot, so shut up and let me carry you."

Since the Zerg queen of white-hot pain and all her little pain-filled broodlings were currently setting up a summer home in my hip, I decided to shut up and let him carry me.

Harper tried to follow us into my bathroom, but I shut the door in her face, muttering something about too many cooks in the kitchen. I hoped I made some kind of sense, but I was in too much pain and panic to care.

I'd used my magic—like a lot of magic. Maybe too much. My head certainly thought I had used way too much. I was out of practice, and I felt like a former athlete who'd spent a couple years on the bench suddenly trying to beat Usain Bolt in the hundred-meter dash.

Plus the more passive side effects of not being human were taking a toll. My body was shoving shards of cell phone and what felt like a million pieces of bullet out of my hip, with what looked like a million gallons of blood.

Alek set me down as gently as he could in my bathtub and then pulled out a knife.

I flinched and held up my hands, but he just sighed and reached for my pants.

"I need to cut those away, take a look."

"Harper," I whispered, then switched to Russian. "She can hear us."

A weird warmth slid over the room, and I watched as the walls took on a slightly silvery sheen.

"No one outside this room can hear anything now," he said.

"Guess being a Justice comes with bonus features."

"First we take care of your wound. Then we'll talk."

I wasn't sure which part of that I looked forward to less. He cut my jeans away and it wasn't anything like the fantasies I hadn't let myself have about him cutting my clothes off. I was too busy trying to seal my teeth to each other with my jaw muscles to tell him that, thank the universe.

With the wound washed off—which, let me tell you was a peachy experience I never want to repeat—it didn't look so bad. Kind of like a steak after you take out your aggression on it with a hammer. And bonus, I now knew what my hipbone looked like and I had a nice collection of metal fragments to show the grandkids. My phone seemed to have eaten the worst of the bullet, and it was super FUBAR.

I lay back in the tub once we got the wound clean, focusing on breathing and not passing out.

"The bleeding has stopped," Alek said. Helpful guy.

"Yeah. Give it a little while. I'll heal." I wished he would shut up and go away.

"You are no hedge witch."

"You are amazing at pointing out obvious things," I said, opening my eyes. "How did you know I'd understand Russian?"

"Call it a hunch."

He leaned against my bathroom counter, looking entirely out of place in the small room. I turned my head, choosing to look at the *Dragon Ball Z* poster I had on the bathroom door instead of into those speculating, piercing blue eyes.

"What happened back there? What kind of magic was that? And how did you save that boy?"

"That's way too many questions for my brain to handle right now," I said. All questions I didn't really want to answer. Some I didn't even have the answer to, anyway. Like what kind of magic this was. Human magic, I was pretty sure, so that meant ritual most likely. But it wasn't like just anybody could use a ritual any more than a kid could open up the *Dungeons & Dragons*

Player's Guide and cast Magic Missile. Magic was everywhere, in everything, but it was like sunlight or carbon molecules. If you don't have the tools to use it and the ability somehow to even tap in, there's no way you can make it work just by trying.

To work a ritual, you'd need knowledge, time, a power source you could access, the right ingredients and foci, combined with a strong enough will to bind it all together. It wasn't those kids, not working alone. Jimmy, the dead one, he'd been on the phone with someone. Someone who had tried to kill both boys using their medallions.

"You are thinking very hard for someone who pretends to know nothing," Alek said, interrupting my half-conscious train of thought.

"I don't know anything, not really. It's all speculation."

Cat-quick, he bent over me and slid his large, warm hand into my shirt. When I pictured him groping my breasts, it wasn't exactly like this. He pulled the medallion out of my bra and dangled it over me. I made out a pattern of circles on its stained black surface and it looked to be molded from clay.

"You pictured me groping your breasts?" he asked, and he had that smirk I'd seen a million years ago this afternoon, before everything went to hell on the handbasket express.

Clearly, I'd spoken aloud. "Blood loss talking," I said. I swiped at the medallion. "Give that back."

"Tell me what it is," he said, standing up out of my reach.

"I don't know." I gave him a smile to show that hey, I could tell the truth sometimes.

"But you can find out." That wasn't even a question. No fair.

"I don't know," I said. "Maybe. Not tonight. I'm kind of in heal mode here. Why don't you go away? I'm rescinding your invitation."

"I am not a vampire." He cocked his head, those ice-chip eyes of his narrowing as he looked me over. "You can't order me out."

"Vampires don't exist," I muttered. I blushed and wondered if I had the blood left in my body for it. I was lying in a bathtub with half my pants missing and only a scrap of black panties covering my girl bits. I wished I'd worn nicer underwear. Or shaved in the last two days. He was a shifter, though, so maybe he preferred his women furry.

Ho-kay. That was definitely the blood loss talking.

I looked down at my hip. The wounds were mostly closed, looking a lot more like a bad abrasion than a bunch of stitch-worthy cuts. Time to get out of the bathtub and find if I had any Band-Aids.

"Still here?" I said. "Help me up."

He pulled me out of the tub as though I were no bigger than a kitten. I lost the scrap of panty but managed to yank a towel over myself as I leaned heavily on the bathroom counter.

"Okay, I need to clean up here, and you really need to leave. Maybe that kid will wake up and tell you what's going on."

He caught my chin in his hand and tilted my head toward him, leaning in close. He smelled like vanilla and sun-kissed hay. "I will come back tomorrow. And you will tell the truth, Jade Crow." All trace of smirk was gone from his face.

"Fuck you," I said, jerking my head away. Mistake, that. Red and black dots swam over my eyes and the headache vise tightened another notch.

"I thought you had revoked my invitation," he said, and just like a freakin' Dr. Jekyll and Mr. Hyde, he was smirking again.

"Do they train you to be this annoying at Justice Academy, or does it come naturally?" I said as I turned carefully around, deliberately not looking in the mirror, and pulled open the medicine cabinet. I did have Band-Aids. Score.

"It runs in my family." He set the medallion down on the counter and pulled open the door. The silvery shield he'd cast on the room dissolved. "I'll be back," he said over his shoulder.

Harper lurked near the door and ducked into the bathroom as soon as Alek left.

"He managed not to make that line sound ironic at all, wow," she said. "What were you guys doing in here?"

"Staring contest," I said. "And I don't think he was actually trying to quote *The Terminator*. You going to sleep over?"

"That okay?" She sounded so young and vulnerable. It was easy to forget sometimes that she was nearly twenty years younger than I was. I might look like I'm in my mid-twenties, but I'm a lot closer to fifty than thirty.

"Of course," I said. "I don't really want to be alone, you know?"

Apparently I wasn't done lying after all.

I didn't want to get up when my alarm blared to life, but the smell of waffles and bacon summoned me. I'd slept fitfully with weird dreams. The final dream ended with the sound of my alarm and the feel of Samir's hands around my throat as he whispered he would be here soon.

For a moment I wondered who was making bacon, but remembered that Harper had slept on my couch. At least she was earning her keep. I sat up too quickly and my hip pinged me with a reminder that I'd been shot the night before. I stumbled to the bathroom with a muttered good morning to Harper and peeled up the Band-Aids.

There was a pretty amazing green, yellow, and purple bruise, but the cuts were all closed. A gaping wound would close within minutes. A bruise? That would stick around for days. Maybe it was my body's way of telling me I should really avoid taking damage.

I pulled on clothes, shared a somewhat awkward and quiet breakfast with Harper, and then went down to open my shop. Harper took her laptop and said she was going to go over to Dr. Lake's and sit with her mother, then she planned to go home and talk to her brother Max about what was happening.

After the craziness of the day before, a quiet day in my shop seemed eerie. I kept waiting for something horrible to happen, but the hours went by without anyone ending up dead or frozen, without any other hot strangers with guns barging in.

Harper called the landline in the shop around four to tell me she was heading to the B&B to talk to Max. I felt weirdly isolated without my cell phone. I ordered a replacement online, but I wouldn't have it until the following Monday.

I had no word from Alek. Ciaran dropped by to say he'd solved everything with the cops, at least for the moment, and that the second kid was in a coma at the hospital. The sheriff was going to write it up as a robbery gone wrong. Nobody had any explanation for how Jimmy had died. It appeared his heart had stopped, just like that. I didn't envy Sheriff Lee her job explaining it to his parents or the admins at the college.

Ezee called the store as well, sometime after when I'd given up on doing inventory and was distracting myself by painting orc miniatures. He said he had recognized one of the kids from school and was going to ask around, see whom they might have associated with. I told him to be careful and asked if he'd seen or heard from the Justice. He hadn't.

The medallion off the kid in the coma was upstairs. As the day faded, I thought about it more and more, trying to anticipate the questions Alek might have and how to answer them in a way that would make sense but not give away more about myself than I already had.

No good. I dropped a mini back onto the newspaper and gritted my teeth.

Thoughts of Samir flooded in. Had even the relatively small amounts of magic I'd used yesterday been too much? Was he even now on his way here to finally kill me? The tracking spell wouldn't register, I didn't think. Way too much ambient magic in this area for that to stand out. But the circle of protection I'd thrown up to fend off whatever killing ritual the shadowy man behind Rose's paralyzing was performing—that wasn't exactly minor magic. I mean, in the scale of things for me, it was. Or it would have been, once upon a time when I was in practice and in shape, magically speaking.

I looked around my shop. Pwned Comics and Games. It was home, the kind of place my teenage self had dreamed about all those years ago after my second family opened my eyes to the world of all that is nerd. I liked my life here. I didn't want things to change. I didn't want to have to run again.

Maybe I was still safe. No more magic, though. Not even my stone-floating exercises, at least not for a while. Whatever happened with Rose and the ritual mage who was behind all this was Alek's problem to handle. He was the one trained for this shit. I could provide emotional support to my friends, but I had to stop being involved.

I could stay for now. Keep my life here. Decision made, I relaxed a little.

Which was when, of course, the universe kicked me in the ass again.

Levi and Harper came through the front door in a rush. I knew it was trouble just from the energy they projected, before I even made out their upset faces and heard a peep from them.

"Ezee is missing," Levi said.

"What do you mean, missing?" I asked. My heart took up residence in my throat.

"He was supposed to meet me at work after his last class got out. He didn't show and he isn't answering either his cell or his office phone."

"Maybe he's at the library? Emergency student conference?" I tried to ignore my painful sense of foreboding.

"Did you talk to him today?" Harper asked.

Shit. "Shit," I said. "I did. He said he knew one of the perps from last night and was going to ask around, see who else might be connected to the guy."

"Shit is right," Levi muttered. "We're going over to Juniper to look for him. Come on."

How could I refuse that? He was my friend. This felt an awful lot like involvement though.

"Where's the Justice?" I asked.

"I think he went to the hospital to see if that guy had woken up yet," Harper said. "He said something about it when he came to check on Mom earlier."

Which meant Alek was at least forty-five minutes away in another town. Wylde wasn't large enough to have a full hospital; we just had the emergency clinic and a couple doctor's offices.

"Okay, let me lock up," I said. What else could I do?

Juniper College is a private liberal arts university known for turning out a lot of serious students who go on to get PhDs and then work in low-level service jobs for the rest of their lives trying to pay off massive student loans. Okay, so maybe not always that last part, but it was one of those elite small schools full of people who seemed more in love with learning than with practical life skills. I'd teased Ezee about it a lot, but in good fun.

I mean, I'd been raised by a bunch of professors and gone to a similar school. Once upon a time I had thought I could be happy in academia for the rest of my life. Before Samir and my wild years as a sorceress-in-training, plotting to make the world my bitch.

The campus was just outside Wylde proper and butted up against the border of the River of No Return Wilderness. Ezee's office was in the oldest building on campus, a beautiful five-story timber and river-stone mansion that sat like a jewel in the middle of a grove of old growth Douglas Fir trees.

The sun was low in the sky when we arrived, the campus quiet in the spring chill. Here and there students walked in packs, talking to each other or with heads buried in their phones, and no one gave us much of a glance.

Ezee's office was on the fourth floor. Levi had a key and let us in when knocking clearly showed his brother wasn't in residence.

Books filled one wall on shelves bending a little under their weight. Two overstuffed leather chairs with brass upholstery tacks decorating them in knotwork patters on the edges were positioned by the desk in a way that invited one in for a cozy chat over a cup of tea about the mysteries of the universe, or, given Ezee's area of expertise, a lively talk about American history and treatment of native peoples.

His desk was orderly, his laptop sitting in sleep mode and plugged into the spike bar on one side. A pile of papers sat waiting to be graded or handed back. There was a pink pen, uncapped, lying on the open area of the desk, as though Ezee had just set it down and was about to return to whatever he'd been writing. Even his desk chair was rotated toward the door, as though he'd only stepped out for a moment, and the Armani aftershave he used still hung in the air.

"Maybe he's in the bathroom? Or we could check the library," I said.

"It feels like he's here. Somehow." Levi shook his head and sniffed the air. "I think he's close. I can't tell. It's like something is blocking my connection to him."

The twins might be fraternal, but shifter twins were an almost unheard of phenomenon. It wasn't a surprise that they were bonded in a magical way. We often joked that if you pinched one, the other would flinch. Or at least glare at you, if it was Levi. Flinching wasn't manly enough for him.

"Do you know his computer password?" Harper asked.

"Is the Pope Catholic?"

"Okay, yeah, stupid question."

Levi sat at the desk and unlocked the laptop. "Nothing immediate that I can see. Let me check his calendar. He writes down everything."

"Can I help you?" A man's voice from right behind me made me jump. Nausea twisted in my gut and I took a step back into the office as I turned and looked the guy over.

He was about my height, maybe five eight, pudgy, close to forty, with thinning brown hair and glasses that exaggerated the bulge of his blue eyes. He wore a brown sweater and a pair of faded khakis and looked utterly unassuming. Yet he set off my creep alert instantly. Maybe it was the nausea. Maybe it was the events of the last day.

"Hi, we're looking for Professor Chapowits," I said. Despite my no-magic vow, I summoned a little of my power and tried to detect if this guy had any magic on him. Nothing. Damn. Maybe I was paranoid.

"He's not here," the man said. "How did you get into his office?" He seemed weirdly nervous, his eyes darting from me, to Harper, to Levi and the computer.

"I'm his brother," Levi said, swinging the chair around. "You are?"

"I'm Bernie uh, Barnes. I work here. That's my office." He jerked a thumb over his shoulder. "Ezekiel is gone for the day. You shouldn't be going through his things."

"He wouldn't have left his laptop, and he'd be answering his phone," Levi said. "Did you see him? What did he say?"

"I just saw him leave a little while ago. Maybe he was getting coffee. He likes to get coffee at the student café. You should try there." Bernie Barnes, whose name sounded like a bad Stan Lee villain, smiled weakly at us, nodding as though he'd thought of something brilliant.

I really didn't like this guy. He seemed desperate to convince us that Ezee wasn't here and everything was fine. I studied him more with my magic enhanced vision. It wasn't that I was getting nothing, I realized. I was seeing not just an absence of magic but an actual null void. He should have registered as a human, with the little ticks and flurries of ambient power that flowed around all life forms. But to my magic-enhanced vision, it was like he wasn't there at all.

"Why don't you come with us," I said. "Show us where it is."

"Okay," Bernie said, surprising me. "Let me lock up my office." He turned and walked down the hall.

"That guy seem weird to you?" Harper asked.

"Hella weird," Levi said.

I stepped out of the office and saw Bernie disappearing not into one of the offices in the hall but through the stairwell doors.

"Shit, he's running," I said.

We bolted after him, Harper and Levi leaving me in their dust as we raced for the stairs. Bernie Barnes flew down those steps ahead of them, outpacing even shifter speed with his lead. Of course, even with super speed, they could only charge down four flights of stairs so quickly.

Make that five flights. Bernie headed for the basement and there we lost him.

The bottom-floor stairway opened into a cramped hall with three doors leading off. No sign of Bernie. The hum of a furnace room greeted me as I slid to a stop beside Harper.

"Which door?" Harper said. She sniffed the air. "I can't smell him. Just dampness."

The air was humid and clammy. I assumed the door with the vents in it was to the mechanical room, so that left two others. Levi pulled open one and revealed a janitorial closet. Not that way. The other door opened to a set of iron stairs that led even further down. We listened at the top of those steps but heard nothing from below over the noise from the old furnace.

"I think that might lead to the steam tunnels. I vote that way." Harper started down the steps.

"Unless he's hiding in the mechanical room waiting for us to go away. Maybe we should split up," Levi said.

"Because splitting the party always leads to win, right?" I said. "Oh, wait, no, it usually leads to death."

"This isn't a game," Levi hissed at me. "My brother could be down there. That guy knows something. He could be the evil behind all this."

"That guy?" Harper said. "But he's so chubby and... nerdy."

"Oh right, so evil can't look like a dopey professor? Do you even read comic books?"

"You trying to accuse me of being a fake nerd girl? Seriously?"

"Hey, you two, stop it." I stepped between them. They were both irritated, their shoulders thrown back, heads forward, posturing like they wanted a fight. Sure, Harper and Levi arguing wasn't unusual but they didn't generally do it in a way that looked like they were about to shift and tear each other apart.

Levi's lips peeled back and his eyes went from dark brown to golden as he gathered his power. He was about to shift.

That was when I sensed the trap. Magic, the same shadowy magic that was binding Rose, coiled around the room like a snake waiting to strike. Waiting for the two shifters to reach into that other world, where their animal selves waited and shift. I had no idea what the trap would do to them. I doubted it would freeze them like Rose—it would take a lot more power than I felt in this room to do something that complicated—but I'd put money on at least knocking them out. It was a pretty hefty spell gathering here.

"*Stop*," I yelled at Levi as Harper growled behind me and Levi tensed to spring.

The trap sprung as he went from man to wolverine in less then a heartbeat. I threw as much power as I could yank up from within myself into another silver circle around all three of us and threw myself into Levi's furry body.

Shadowy power swirled around my circle and then dissipated with a discordant chime that rang inside my head as I held onto the image of a silver protecting circle even as I tried to hold back a wolverine almost as big as I was. Levi's claws ripped into my back and then he was a man again, holding me instead of me holding him.

"Shit. Jade. Shit. I'm so sorry." Levi shook in my arms as he pulled away and then reached out again, his hands bloody.

"It's okay. It was a trap," I managed to say.

"Jade. Your back," Harper said. She knelt behind me and reached for the shreds of my shirt.

"It's not so bad," I said, though it felt pretty unfun. The pain was not the white-hot stab of the bullet wound the night before but a more twisting ache. I'd already used too much magic warding off and diffusing the trap. What was a little more? I called on more power and it came even easier than the day before, my sorceress skills apparently not as rusty as I'd thought. I sealed myself off from the pain, pushing power at the wounds and imagining I was a cleric casting a cure moderate wounds spell.

"Shit," Harper said. "How did you do that?"

"You aren't a hedge witch," Levi said softly, staring at me with a mix of awe and fear on his face.

"No. I'll explain later," I said. I wouldn't. I had to leave Wylde, like, yesterday. It wasn't safe here anymore.

But first I'd go down into those steam tunnels with them and see if we could find Ezee. If there were more traps, well, what was a little extra magic? Samir wouldn't be here in the next hour.

I hoped.

"Come on. Let's go see what's down those steps," I said, getting to my feet.

Levi unzipped his hoodie and handed it to me. I pulled it on over my ruined shirt and felt like crying. My friends were good people. I was going to miss them like crazy. But I'd rather miss them than get them killed.

"Gamers in steam tunnels. This always ends well," I said, trying to smile.

Neither of them smiled back.

The steps led down into a tight corridor. The clamminess increased, and as we moved carefully forward, the air took on the faint scent of decay.

The corridor branched. Levi sniffed and motioned to the right. Even I could tell the smell of dead things was stronger that way. We didn't speak. My head started pounding, and it was difficult to breathe as the stench escalated.

The tunnel terminated in a round room that had probably held more mechanical devices for moving warm air around the place fifty or a hundred years ago. Now it just held a room out of a B-movie horror flick.

A huge pentagram was drawn on the floor in what looked like brownish paint but was probably dried blood. On a metal shelf to one side was an assortment of dried herbs, a couple ritual daggers straight out of a Kit Rae catalog complete with gem skulls and extraneous spiked bits, and a few books about magic. The books were bunk, new-age and totally harmless. Yet somehow this guy and his flunkies had managed to raise a lot of power. On the other side of the pentagram was a desk with a few papers strewn across it and beyond that another door.

"Oh God," Harper moaned. She'd walked over to the desk and stood with her arms wrapped protectively around herself.

I moved to where I could see past her and the desk and found the source of the dead animal smell.

Two wolves were crouched there, both frozen like Rose, snarls on their faces. They were far too large to be real wolves, I realized. They had been shifters. One was rotted away, bones clearly sticking out in yellowed contrast to the grey fur. Its eyes were gone, only dark, gunky sockets remained.

The other wolf was in slightly better shape. Its body was emaciated, looking like a creature out of a Humane Society commercial but even worse. Patches of its fur had come off, and I could count its ribs and just about every other bone in its body. Its dark brown eyes were still there, staring up at us.

"I think Ezee was here," Levi whispered, coming up beside Harper and I. "I can faintly smell him."

"They are dead, right? Not like Mom," Harper said. I wasn't sure she was talking to me, but I put my hand gently on her shoulder anyway.

"That smell certainly says so," I said. I looked down at the desk. "Hey, is that a map?" Maybe we'd finally caught a break here.

"Yeah. That's a map of the Frank near the Wylde river region here." Levi bent over the map, tracing the lines. "Guess he got out in too much of a hurry to take it. Wonder what this writing is."

I studied the writing. "Sanskrit?" I guessed. "It's notes about the full moon hitting zenith and some kind of conjunction with Jupiter. Those lines there that look random? Those are ley lines, I think. He's mapped out a node of power there. That can't be good."

"How many languages do you speak?" Levi was staring at me again.

"All of them."

"No, seriously," he said.

See? Even when I tell the truth, no one believes me. What's the point?

"Is Mom going to end up like that?" Harper said. Her eyes were locked on the wolves.

"No, Harper, geez. Don't even think like that. We've uncovered a huge lead for Alek, right?" I gave her shoulder a little shake.

"The full moon is tonight," Levi said.

"We have to find Alek," I said. "Come on, that guy is long gone and I don't want us lost down here. We know where he will be. Bring the map and stuff."

"Are you sure they are dead?" Harper said, refusing to be pulled away as Levi gathered up the papers on the desk.

Oh for fuck's sake. I swallowed the words and walked around the desk, breathing only through my mouth as my eyes watered under the assault of the bodies' acrid smell. I bent and put my hand on the head of the wolf that was less rotted out and summoned up my magic again.

The same twisting dark bonds that had locked Rose up were present in the wolf. Same pattern, same flow toward an intricate knot I could sense but not unravel.

Same faint heartbeat beneath it.

I stumbled back too quickly and ended up on my ass against the wall. I knew what Bernie Barnes was up to. I knew where all his power was coming from. The emaciated bodies filled in the final puzzle piece.

It shouldn't have been possible, but somehow he had found a way to paralyze shifters and then cannibalize their innate power for his own spells.

"He's not dead, is he? He's like Mom. That's what Mom is gonna be. No, no," Harper cried out, and started to come around the desk.

"Get her out of here, Levi," I said, shoving myself to my feet. "I'll meet you guys at the car. Go!"

Levi's eyes met mine and he nodded gravely, understanding what I meant to do. He grabbed Harper's arm and yanked her toward the door we'd come in. "Come on, kid. We need to get out of here."

Tears streaming down her face, she looked at me and then nodded bleakly.

I waited until they were through the door and out of sight before I walked over to the shelf and picked up one of the daggers. I wanted to cuss Alek and his stupid fucking visions right out, but it wasn't him who had done this. His vision was about to come true, in a way, but it was my choice. I'm good at lying and at running, but I try not to lie to myself too much. It's a bad habit.

I stood over the wolf, my hand shaking as I held the dagger. I knew I should drive it into the wolf's heart. Which would make me a killer.

Warmth spread through me as a furry head butted into my side, rocking me on my feet. Wolf, my guardian, materialized beside me and nudged my arm again. I looked at her through blurred vision. The tears I'd been trying to shed in the last two days were here finally, stinging as they ran down my cheeks.

"Okay," I whispered, "Message received."

I knelt and drove the dagger into the wolf's chest.

We didn't have to track Alek down. He was waiting for us outside the game shop when we arrived after a silent and tense car ride.

"We know who it is."

"He has Ezee."

"He has my brother."

All three of us spoke on top of each other, and Alek held up a hand.

"One at a time, and maybe not out here?" He looked at me and frowned. "I smell blood."

"I'm fine," I said. I pulled out my keys, bumping my bruised hip as I did so. Another painful reminder that I wasn't fine. Nothing was. Again I felt irrational anger at Alek for coming into my world and wrecking everything.

Two days ago everything had been normal. Now, my life was ruined. Again.

Inside the shop, Levi and I quickly explained what had happened at the school. I pushed the miniatures to the side and Levi laid out the map we'd found. Harper sat heavily in my chair behind the desk and booted up my computer.

"Think he actually works there? We can find out who he really is on the faculty page, I think," she said. Her face was too calm, her eyes puffy but clear. She had the hollow look of someone who had suffered too much pain too quickly and burned down to an empty core of rage.

I knew that feeling. I knew that look. Intimately. I was halfway there myself. The other half? Sheer terror.

"I'm going upstairs to get a new shirt," I said.

Alek followed me. I wasn't really surprised.

"If we are going to talk," I said, "Then you better do that silence-ward thingy you did last night." Fuck. Only last night I'd been bleeding in my bathtub. Two nights ago I'd been plotting how to sucker my players into their latest adventure and rolling up stats on a Lich Lord.

Silvery magic slipped over the walls of my bedroom. I pulled out a batman tee-shirt and pulled off the bloody hoodie and my torn up shirt. I kept my back to Alek and he waited until I was clothed again before speaking.

"This Bernie Barnes, he's a sorcerer like you?" he asked.

So, he had figured out what I was. Guess that wasn't really a surprise.

"No. He's using rituals, which I guess makes him a warlock. The magic isn't inside him; he's stealing it. I think that's what the ley-line map and his notes are about." I sat heavily on my bed and looked down at my hands. There was dried blood under my nails. Awesome. Tears threatened again. Twenty-plus years without crying and now I was about to do it twice in a day. More awesome.

"Stealing power from shifters," Alek prompted. "Like a sorcerer."

"Stop saying that. You're wrong. We can't steal power, not like that." I glared at him. "I have power because I was born with it. It's like this well inside me. A witch or warlock or whatever you call a human magic user has only the ability to use power, not the actual power itself inside them. They have to do special rituals or tap power sources like ley lines, bodies of water, or plots of land, Gods, that kind of thing, to actually work magic. Shifters are different. You guys are one-trick ponies. Well, you might not be." I stopped for a steadying breath and waved my hand at my shimmering walls. "But most shifters just have that one connection to their animal.

You guys *are* magic, instead of using it. And it isn't a magic that is accessible to anyone else. If I ate your heart, nothing would happen but a bad stomach ache."

"You eat hearts? I thought that was legend." He ran a hand through his hair. Some fell over his forehead and I wanted to get up and go to him, brush it away. Lean into his vanilla and musk warmth and pretend he was just a hot guy in my bedroom and that I wasn't sitting here on borrowed time while the world went to ruin around me.

"I don't," I said. "But I could. If, say, I ate the heart of this Bernie guy, I'd have his knowledge, his ability to use the kind of power he's wielding." I saw Alek's expression at that and realized I really shouldn't have used this situation as an example. "Anyway, that's a sorcerer thing. Bernie can't do that. I think—and again, I'm making educated but pretty crazy guesses with the stuff we already know—he's not using shifter powers so much as using their life force as a source. He's doing it with shifters probably for a couple reasons. One, no one is going to be that alarmed if they come across a guy with a bunch of stuffed animals lying around. Two, you guys have a lot of life source. What makes you hard to kill is what makes you perfect as a sort of magical battery for this guy."

Now that I was saying it all aloud it made even more sense than it had in my head as I ran through my ideas on the drive back to my shop.

"The full moon, the ley-line node, and a fresh, healthy shifter to power whatever he's doing out there tonight... Well, put it together and you've got really bad news. He might be able to tap into the node from there and create some kind of permanent conduit. After that, and considering how he views your kind as walking batteries, you'll have a serious problem."

"Yes," Alek said. "But we can stop him tonight, before the moon rises. Make him undo what he has done. And then I'll kill him."

"Wait, what's this 'we', white man?" I said. "I am not going with you. And don't you dare drag Levi and Harper along either. They nearly got caught in one of this guy's traps today. You have training, experience. They don't. Right now this guy is pretty much just a human. You should be able to handle that." Though we had no idea how many minions he had left. Two were out of commission. Were there more? I shoved the thought into the *not my problem* file.

"Why not come with me? You have power and you can help stop him—do your protection thing and tell me if he's undoing his magic."

"No. I'm leaving town before I get us all killed." He'd been right when he told me the night before that I would tell him the truth. He already knew what I was. What did it matter if he knew the rest? "I'm here in Wylde because I thought the ley lines and the abundance of shifters and other magic users would hide me. But it was only going to work as long as I didn't use my own magic. All those horror stories you hear about sorcerers? They aren't really about the rest of us, few as we are. They are about one man and he's probably on his way here right now to destroy me and anyone I care about."

"Then I will fight him with you, in exchange for your help on this current matter." Alek looked skeptical, and his shrug was overly casual.

I laughed, the sound raw and ugly. I could have left it at that; he didn't need to understand, after all. I didn't need to change his mind. But I wanted him to know the truth—it was weirdly important to me that he see I was right, that I couldn't stay, how badly I had to run. It wasn't only terror making me go; it was the only way anyone would survive.

"Wolf, show him," I said softly, looking over at where my guardian was flopped on the floor by my dresser. Alek gave me a strange look, which was fair, since as far as he could see I was talking to an empty patch of carpet.

Then he gasped and his hand slid to his gun as Wolf chose to become visible. She was all black, the size of a pony, with a wolf's head and ears, a body like a tiger's, giant paws with retractable claws like a lynx's, and the long, thick tail of a snow leopard. Her eyes were the black of a perfect night sky with no moon, their depths endless and full of tiny stars.

"Undying," he murmured, and for a moment I thought he might bow or something. "She is with you?" He looked at me with something like awe on his face.

Wolf was a spirit guardian, what some called the Undying. The legend went that they were the guards of the beings that had become the human's gods. I don't really know about that, since Wolf doesn't talk to me and certainly doesn't share any secrets of the universe with me.

"I guess so. My cousins dropped me down a mine shaft as a bad joke when I was four. I was hurt and terrified, but then Wolf showed up. She stopped the pain and carried me out. Been with me ever since." I stood up and went to her. "But that isn't what I wanted you to see." I touched her belly where a stark white line of scar tissue broke up the perfect darkness of her fur.

"Samir, the sorcerer after me, he did that to her last time I ran from him."

"He scarred an Undying?" Alek gave a low whistle.

"He's been gathering power and eating the hearts of any rivals since back when a guy named Jesus told the meek they'd inherit the earth," I said. "Now do you see? You want me to help you stop the magical equivalent of a drunk driver while I'm telling you I need to get the hell out of here before I bring down a world-ending meteor on our heads."

Wolf butted me with her head and then disappeared. No idea what she meant by that gesture, as usual. I chose to ignore the feeling of unhappiness I got from it.

"So you will keep running from him." Alek's tone made it clear that wasn't a question. "Until when?" That was probably rhetorical.

I ignored his tone. "Until I'm strong enough to fight him."

"And you grow stronger while you run away?" Alek said in a tone I was starting to really hate.

"I don't know. He's evil, Alek, and he hates me with an obsessive rage. He hunted me down after I failed to kill him the first time, used my family to lure me out. He would have killed all of us if I hadn't run." Tears sprang to my eyes and I curled my hands into fists. "He killed them. Because of me."

Technically, they'd killed themselves after he'd captured and tortured them and then hooked them up to a bomb. I could still hear Ji-hoon's last words telling me not to come, telling me to flee as far and as fast as I could. Could hear the sound of the bomb as the four of them decided they would rather give their lives by setting the device off than let Samir take me as well.

"You tried to kill him?"

"Dammit. Yes. I found out he wasn't really my lover or my friend. He was using me, fattening up my magic by training me and helping me be more powerful so he could make a tastier meal of me later. So yeah, I tried to kill him. I failed, okay? Twice. And now, this is my life. I run away so that I can live. So that my friends here can live."

"I understand," he said. His voice had gone cold and quiet. "I will go stop this warlock myself."

He turned and walked to the door, throwing it open as he dropped his soundproofing ward. Then he hesitated and looked back at me.

"You survive," he said. "Not live. You are not living, Jade Crow."

"Fuck you," I yelled after him. I didn't need his judgment. Anger would have been better than the disappointment in his face. Better than those words, words so close to the ones my own heart whispered to me in the dead hours of the night sometimes.

I stumbled into the bathroom and saw the medallion sitting on the counter where I'd apparently forgotten it the night before. I shoved it into a drawer. I turned the water on as hot as I could stand and scrubbed at my hands until no more blood stained them. Then I splashed water on my face until I could look into the mirror and pretend I didn't look like a mess.

Levi and Harper were still in the shop, alone. I let out my breath with a huff of relief. At least Alek had made them stay here.

"That guy told us the truth," Levi said. "His name really is Bernard Barnes and he's a professor of Religious Studies at Juniper."

"Well, I guess that's good," I said. My brain was already inventorying the place, trying to decide what I would take with me and what I would leave. I'd have to leave most of it.

"He said you weren't going to help," Harper said. She came around from behind the counter and stood, hands on her hips, looking at me with accusing green eyes.

"I'd get in the way," I said.

"That's what he said about us." Harper shook her head.

"He's right, Harper. He's a Justice. They are like super-shifters, right? That's what you guys told me. Your Council of Nine sent him here to fix things. So let him do his job."

"She's right," Levi said, his voice rough but soft. "Let's go, Harper."

I was glad to have support from his quarter, but it surprised me. I squinted at him. "Where are you going?"

"To see Mom at Dr. Lake's. Max is with her. If that's okay with you?" She said the last part with an exaggerated sneer.

Fuck. My last conversation with my best friend was going to be a fight. Totally awesomesauce. Not.

"Yeah, of course," I said. I went to her and tried to give her a hug.

She stepped back. "See you later," she said. Levi was already half out the door.

"Bye, guys," I whispered as the door chimes rang.

How do you leave a home? If the third time was supposed to be the charm, one would think I'd have this down by now.

I locked up my shop and went back upstairs. A couple pairs of jeans, the few teeshirts I hadn't bled on and destroyed in the last couple days, socks, underclothes, my Pikachu footie pajamas. I didn't take any of my posters or figurines, but I did pack my dice bag. I knew wherever I went, I could probably find gamers. We are legion, after all.

I did my dishes and vacuumed all the floors. I was walking out on my lease, so I figured the least I could do was clean up the place a bit. I looked around. This was my life. And now it was over. Again.

I walked down into the shop and flicked on a light. My orc miniatures sat on the counter, primed and ready for paint to bring them to life. I could almost hear the echo of my friends' laughter from the back room where the game table stood empty, could smell the traces of a hundred pizza deliveries and spilled soda pop. The concrete floors were scuffed around the counter where Harper's combat boots always left marks when she stood there for hours on end chatting away with me while playing Hearthstone on her laptop.

I walked behind the counter and took a single framed picture off the wall. It was the only thing I still had from my last real home, twenty years ago.

It was just a pen sketch. Four figures done up comic-book style and a small Korean signature in red ink at the bottom. Ji-hoon, one of my surrogate parents, had been an illustrator for Marvel back in the Comics Bronze Age of the late seventies and eighties. He'd done a family portrait for me as a high school graduation present.

There was Kayla with her usual side ponytail and giant smile. Sophie with her 1980s punk band Mohawk and one hand flipping off the artist. Todd with his hair over his forehead, his oversized glasses, and his favorite Pi teeshirt on. Ji-hoon with his carefully cut black hair, and slight stature that he always exaggerated in self-portraits. And an awkward girl named Jessica Carter with waist-length black hair, big cheekbones, and a huge glowing D20 pendant around her neck.

That had been me. I'd been Jade Crow when I was born. Then Jessica Carter to my second family. Jade Crow again to my third.

I didn't know who I would be next. I just wanted to be myself, whoever that was. But I'd chosen the wrong boyfriend in college, and any normal life after that was game over for me. Alek had been right about that. I had to be in survival mode, always. I'd forgotten that truth these last few years, making a home here in Wylde.

I'd been stupid.

"And this, kids, is why we can't have nice things," I said to the picture before tucking it into my duffle bag.

I looked around again. Dammit. I didn't want to leave. Maybe my car wouldn't start and I'd be stuck. Maybe Samir had given up on me. The last time he'd gotten anywhere near me that I knew of was over a decade ago. Maybe he wasn't still looking for my magical signature, waiting to trap me. Maybe he was dead.

Fat fucking chance.

I had to leave. Tonight. Putting it off would make leaving tougher. My friends were pissed at me. I was pissed at me. Would using more magic to help Alek have been so awful?

I wasn't sure. I didn't trust what I might do if faced with a choice between saving Rose and Ezee and letting them die.

Alek had said his vision showed me standing at a crossroads between shifters dying and living. I'd killed one shifter, a man whose name I might never know. It didn't matter it that it was a mercy killing. I didn't want to kill anyone.

Lies. I wanted to kill Samir. Sometimes I dreamed terrible and explicit revenge fantasies when I couldn't sleep on the worst nights. I wanted to rain hell upon him in the worst way. And yet. He had a couple thousand years of practice on me and only in my deepest nightmares did I even speculate how many sorcerers and human mages he'd eaten over the millennia. There was no way I'd ever be strong enough to face him.

And you grow stronger while you run away? Alek's words ran through my mind.

I hadn't grown stronger. The magic I had used in the last two days felt pretty weak to me. My power was still there, but I'd grown out of shape, out of practice. I was getting weaker.

"All the more reason you can't stay," I said aloud to the accusing silence. Maybe I was a coward, but I'd be an *alive* coward. And my friends would be safe. I was doing the right thing.

I sighed and wondered whom I was trying to convince, standing here arguing with myself in my head about a decision that only had one good answer where everyone got to go on living.

Survive. You are not living, Jade Crow. Alek's words in my head again.

Footsteps raced up the street outside, distracting me from my stupid inner turmoil, and I was already turning toward the door when Max, Harper's little brother, ran into it and started yelling my name.

I unlocked the door and Max nearly fell into my arms as he burst through, talking rapidly.

"Woah there, buddy. Slow down. Who took Rose?" I tried to parse his rushed sentences.

"Harper and Levi," he said. "They came by a while ago, said I should go get some coffee. I went out and when I got back nobody was there. They took Mom. I thought I should run to you cause your phone just goes to voicemail and no one is picking up and I don't know where they are."

"I do," I muttered, thinking hard. Levi had definitely given in too easily. "Idiot."

"Me?"

"No, not you. Me. I should have known they'd go after Alek. They're going to try to fight the guy who did that to your mom and force him to undo it."

“Good,” Max said.

“What? No. Not good.” They were going to go get in the way at best, and at worst get Alek killed if he was distracted trying to protect them. They’d get everyone killed, or enslaved and paralyzed, and universe knew what else. Fucking toast on a stick.

I had to stop them. Or save them. I couldn’t just leave now.

Besides, I really *did* want to fight something. Bernard Barnes wasn’t Samir, but he was a start.

Maybe this was the universe’s way of telling me it was time to stop running.

“All right, Universe,” I said, glaring up at the ceiling. “Message received.”

“What are you going to do?” Max said as he followed me up the steps and into my apartment.

“I know sort of where they were going, but we don’t have the map. So I have to cast a spell on this medallion I took off one of the evil minions so we can track the person who made it, who I bet is the guy your sister and Levi went after, and so we can stop him from killing everyone before the moon hits zenith.”

“Cool,” Max said.

Oh, to be fifteen again.

The medallion was still in the bathroom drawer. I looked it over, finding little imperfections and dents in the clay that I hoped meant it was handmade. The stain on it reminded me of dried blood, and I tried not to think about that too hard as I held it in both hands and called on my magic.

It was a variation of the spell I'd done for Alek, only I needed no compass this time. The medallion would act as my guide. I felt it pulling northwest.

"You have your permit, right?" I asked Max as we descended the stairs to my car. The moon was already peaking up over the buildings.

"Yeah?"

"Good." I tossed him my keys. "I need to focus on this spell. You're driving. Try not to kill us."

For the record, my car started up just fine.

"Pull over here," I told Max after about half an hour of driving on the narrow highway along the border of the River of No Return Wilderness. "This is where I have to go on foot."

"The moon is over the trees," he said as we got out of the car. "How far is it? How long do we have?"

I almost said, "Who is this 'we,' white man," but I'd used that line once today and I figured there was some kind of cosmic limit.

"Me. I'm going. You are staying here with my car and making sure it doesn't get stolen."

"Stolen. Right." His shoulders slumped.

"I mean it, Max. Please?" I softened my tone and gave him my best desperate female gaze.

"Okay," he muttered.

I followed the medallion's pull into the trees, shoving my way through the undergrowth. It was goddamned dark in here. I used more magic, feeding it into my talisman until the D20 glowed enough that I could see a few feet ahead. The ferns and weeds grew fewer as I moved into the more mature forest away from the road, but I was still moving too slowly. My lungs hurt and my leg muscles burned as I half stumbled, half ran through the dark woods.

This wasn't working. At this rate, I'd get there about dawn if they were really deep into the wilderness. There might have been an access road or old logging path that provided a better way, but my tracking spell wasn't Google Maps. It could only tell me direction, not the best route by car.

How long had it been since Alek and company stormed out of my store? Two hours? Three? Maybe they'd won and were on their way back to rub in my face how I'd missed all the action.

"Stop talking yourself out of doing shit," I said aloud as I stopped moving for a moment and leaned against a tree. I wasn't sure about lovely, but the woods were dark and deep. Robert Frost had gotten that part right. I guess two of three ain't bad. Wind rustled in the branches high over my head as I gasped in the cool, damp air.

Wolf materialized beside me and cocked her head at me.

"You going to help?" I asked her, not expecting an answer.

She bent low and twisted her head toward her back.

"Guess that's a yes," I said, smiling at her. "Thank you." I jumped up onto her back, digging my free hand into her thick, warm fur and clinging with my sore legs. I hadn't ridden on Wolf's back since she'd dragged us both bleeding and half dead out of the burning rubble where my family had chosen death and where I'd made my second and most disastrous stand against Samir.

This ride was a lot more fun. She sprang forward, gliding just over the ground in large, smooth bounds. I kept my grip on her fur and on the medallion, holding the tracking spell as best I could, but she seemed to know where to go. We soared through the woods, covering miles in a rush. I finally gave up on the spell and used that hand to grip my braid, keeping my head down as branches whipped by and threatened to tear off all my hair. Long hair can be a bitch.

After an eternity that wasn't long enough, Wolf slowed and dropped into a crouch. As my ears adjusted to the sudden lack of movement and wind, I heard chanting coming from up ahead. I blinked tears from my eyes and peered into the darkness. There seemed to be more light in front of us than a full moon on a clear night could account for.

Wolf crept forward until she reached the edge of a giant clearing where the trees stopped abruptly and the land sloped downward. In the moonlight I saw a field at the bottom of the hill. Tiki torches were set in a loose ring, providing enough light to make out what was going on.

There were no triumphant friends or even a raging battle. As far as I could tell, my side had already pretty much lost whatever fight had happened.

Within the ring of light were two circles drawn with what I guessed was loose chalk. The smaller circle held a huge white tiger. Alek, I guessed. He was caught within a holding spell, I assumed, since he should have been able to just step out of the thing but instead was turning and growling as though he were caught in an iron cage.

The second, larger circle contained Bernie Barnes in a ridiculous black hooded robe with silver runes sewn onto it. He knelt over a reddish-brown dog. No, not a dog. A coyote. Ezee. Barnes was chanting in Sanskrit, the words much less relevant than the twisting shadow lines of power swirling like ghosts above him.

For a moment I didn't see Harper or Levi. Maybe Max had been wrong. I scanned the ground inside the ring of torches, and two dark shapes on the edge caught my eye. A fox and a wolverine, red and fawn fur bright against the dark grass. I couldn't tell from here if they were alive, but they definitely weren't conscious.

Rage swelled in me, white hot, and with it came more of my magic. I fed my frustration into it, and gathered power in my hands.

"All right, Wolf," I whispered to my companion, "the plan is we charge down there and wreck that motherfucker's night."

I couldn't kill him, since we needed him to undo his spells, but I could make him hurt. Make him regret ever even thinking about using magic. I could show him what a real goddamn mage could do.

Wolf charged. We burst down the hill and into the ring of torches, and I brought my hands up, aiming balls of force right at Bernie's hooded head.

I totally would have saved the night if the evil minion I hadn't spotted had waited just another few seconds.

But he didn't.

Instead he shot me in the back.

The shot was loud. The bullet ripped through me and the pain wiped my grip on my magic. That whole thing with the bullet in the hip? A flesh wound compared to the tearing pain that spiked through my chest. I think I stopped breathing.

I tumbled off Wolf's back and stopped my fall with my face. My arms and legs didn't seem to want to respond. I didn't think a bullet could kill a sorceress, but this one felt like it was giving an A-plus effort.

The pain turned from lightning strikes to a deep, terrifying chill. I heard the chanting continue, and beside me Wolf growled. She might look scary as fuck, but she can't actually do anything to a human. Or stop a bullet.

My eyes didn't seem to want to open, either. The grass was wet and cool on my cheek. Maybe I'd just stay here. It smelled good. Clean. Nothing like blood or dying animals. I don't like blood. It's so sticky.

"I got her!" a man's voice called out near me.

Wolf licked my back, her tongue molten hot, and I screamed. The pain faded back enough that I could think again, and when I moved my hands to get them underneath me and pry my face off the dirt, they sluggishly obeyed.

I raised my head, spitting out blood and dirt. My mouth was gritty but at least my eyes were working now and I seemed to be able to breathe again. A young man in a black robe stood about ten feet from me, pointing a gun and grinning.

I reached for my magic, and this time I didn't try to really control the flow of it. I tore open the dams on my power and let it fill me to the brim. The pain gave up, turning off like a switch had been flipped. I knew somewhere in my subconscious that I was going to really regret this tomorrow, but I wanted to live until tomorrow.

I wrapped one hand around my talisman and struggled to my knees. I thrust my magic down into my left arm and used it to extend my fist, slapping the gun out of the evil minion's hand. He yelled in surprise, but I didn't stop there. I swung my arm back, using the same force to punch him in the face.

He went down and stayed down. Guess no one had ever told him not to bring a gun to a mage fight.

I laughed, though the sound came out as more of a hiccupping cough. The chanting grew quicker, more frantic. I twisted and looked at Bernie. The moonlight shone on the huge silver dagger in his hands as he raised it over Ezee's body. He was twenty feet away from me at least. I tried to rise and my vision swam with red and black dots.

Tiger-Alek roared, drawing my gaze to him. He was closer. I remembered how quickly he could move. He just needed out of that circle.

That, I could do.

I let go of my talisman and slammed both fists into the ground, channeling the raging tide of my magic into the surface of the earth. I visualized it charging just under the roots of the grass like a tunneling *Arrakis* sandworm. The grass rippled and the earth buckled in a straight line from my hands to the circle trapping Alek.

When the ripple hit the circle, I yanked my fists up and threw them wide in a breaking motion.

The circle flew apart, dark shards of power shooting into the air and chalk exploding in a white cloud. Tiger-

Alek sprang free and took two great leaping bounds before he crashed through the circle surrounding Bernie.

"Don't kill him!" I yelled. My magical tide was receding. I was definitely hitting a limit. I pushed myself to my feet.

Tiger-Alek slammed into Bernie, knocking him to the side. Then he was just Alek again. He grabbed the chubby warlock by his robe and twisted his wrist in a crazy Bruce Lee kind of move until Bernie screamed and dropped the knife. Even stumbling forward and still fifteen feet away, I heard Bernie's arm break.

"Is the spell broken?" Alek called to me.

I looked around. No more shadows flew around the broken circle, and though I could still sense Bernie's weird, nauseating magic, it wasn't strong anymore.

"I think so," I said. "Harper? Levi?"

"Alive. I can hear them breathing."

Super senses must be nice. I sagged with relief.

"Good. So, Bernie Barnes, we meet again." I looked down at the whimpering man. He looked so pathetic that I almost felt sorry for him. Almost.

"You don't understand," he whined. "You don't know what you've done. I was so close."

"I. Don't. Fucking. Care," I said. "Save the Bond villain explanation for whatever god greets you in hell. Unless, of course, you want to live."

There was zero way he was going to live. Shifter justice isn't very nice. But he didn't need to know that yet.

"Yes," he said, his bug-like blue eyes filled with desperation.

"All you have to do is undo your spells, the ones that suck power from my friends. Very simple." I smiled at him.

From his reaction, it wasn't a very pleasant smile.

"I, uh," he stuttered, and then looked up at Alek and then back at me. "I can't."

"You worked the spell. How?"

"I found an old book. Bought it on eBay. Most of it was gibberish, but then some of the spells worked. But I couldn't get enough power, not from people. They kept dying, you see. Then I discovered one of them." He looked back up at Alek. "Werepeople. The book described using magical creatures as vessels."

"Where is this book?" And what fucking idiot warlock had written down such dangerous spells? Rage trickled back through me, giving me a second wind, and I glared down at the shaking man.

"I burnt it. I didn't want my disciples to steal it. Jimmy and Collin were always lifting things, trying to find ways to gain power like I did. Then they sold that damn fox for weed money. This is their fault!"

"Oh yeah, your problem was that you hired bad help. Sure." I looked at Alek. His eyes were flame and ice in the flickering torchlight.

"He's telling the truth," Alek said softly.

"So you can't undo your spells? You really don't know how?"

"No, I'm telling you. The book didn't tell me that. Why would I want to? Before now, I mean. Those two," he said, motioning toward Harper and Levi, "they aren't tapped. They are just unconscious. They'll wake up. See? It's only that one."

"Not just him," I said. "What about the fox? What about those wolves under your office?"

"I can't do anything about it now. Don't let that thing kill me. I won't do it again. I'm sorry," Bernie said, his voice rising into a high screech.

I sank to my knees and reached out for Ezee's body beside me, sliding my hand into his soft brown fur. Shadow bonds wrapped around him in the same twisting pattern they did on Rose. I found his heartbeat, faint but there.

"This is the crossroads," I whispered, looking up at Alek. "This is what you saw."

He just stared down at me, not moving, his face giving nothing away. I knew somehow that he would let me decide. That if I said the word, he'd become the Justice once more and execute the sentence of death on Bernie Barnes.

That was one path, one road leading away from the junction I now metaphorically stood at. Down that path, Bernie died. Rose and Ezee also died. Slowly and horribly, or else they would have to be put down by friends. By me, or maybe Alek. I wasn't going to ask Harper or Levi to do it.

On that path, they died.

There was another path.

"No, Bernie," I said, the words falling like stones from my mouth. "You won't do it again." I summoned my magic, fighting the pounding exhaustion that threatened to stem the flow.

Then I plunged my hand, cloaked in raw power, into Bernie's chest and ripped out his heart.

I didn't let myself think about what I was doing. I just acted, shoving the bleeding hunk of muscle into my mouth and biting down hard. I didn't know if I had to eat the whole thing or not. I hoped not. It was hot and tough, like trying to chew a raw steak. I ripped off the biggest piece I could and swallowed it without chewing more than once, half choking, and I fought to not immediately vomit it back up.

Shadowy power exploded in my chest as I swallowed and a flood of images and impressions overloaded my mind. Ugly, jock-type boys gathered around me, taunting me for my glasses, my weird name. Learning Sanskrit. Stabbing a shadowy knife into a screaming man's chest. Cinnamon rolls. Shadow power welling inside me as young men sat at my feet, eager to learn. I think I passed out as Bernie's life and mine collided.

Then the sensory overload stopped, and just like that I was awake. My head was clear and this strange new knowledge was there, as though I'd downloaded a new file to the desktop of my brain.

I reached for Ezee, the shadow bonds inside him clear as lines on a map to me now. I knew what they were for, how they leeched his life force and transmuted it into an energy I now knew how to use.

I was relieved that the very idea of this still nauseated the fuck out of me.

I unraveled the bonds. I didn't need a book to understand how this magic worked. Now that I could touch it, control it, my sorceress abilities took over and bent it to my will. I snapped the bonds, unwinding the knot around his heart.

He came alive with a yelp and sprang up. Then he shifted, turning instantly from coyote back to a man.

"Jade," he said, and then looked past me and ran for his twin's inert form.

I didn't take it personally. He could thank me later. All I wanted to do now was pass out and sleep for maybe a couple million years. The rush of new power was fading, leaving me hollow. The pain in my chest came back with an insistent throb and spots danced in my vision again. Not enough spots, though, to keep me from turning and seeing Bernie's dead body lying in a black heap on the bloody grass. I felt nothing but a faint sadness for the man he could have been if he'd chosen another path.

I decided I could process later. It was definitely past time to be unconscious. On cue, Alek lifted me into his impossibly strong arms.

"Max," I said. "He's out there, at the highway. Someone should call him."

"Shh," he murmured. "I'll handle it from here."

He was warm, so warm. My skin felt rimed with ice in comparison. I nuzzled my head into his shoulder, pressing my bruised nose to his chest.

"You smell good," I said.

And then, because the Universe can sometimes be a merciful bitch, I passed the fuck out.

It took me three days before I could do more than stumble to the bathroom and sip orange juice. I managed to pull up enough power at some point after I woke up the first day to free Rose from Bernie's spell. Doing so knocked me out again right afterwards.

I don't know what Alek said to the evil minion who'd shot me. I decided I wouldn't ask. He'd shot me, after all. I also had no idea what happened to Bernie's body, but I was willing to bet it would never be found. The boy in the coma woke up after I killed Bernie and fled town. Without the book and without Bernie to teach them, I figured he was probably harmless now.

Unfortunately, the spell that had bound Rose and Ezee didn't put them to sleep. They'd both been awake and aware the entire time. Rose told us how she'd been approached by two young men who had said they were lost while hiking and how they'd lured her into one of Bernie's magical traps. The boy in the coma had stolen her from Bernie and sold her to Ciaran after he and Bernie argued about how they weren't learning useful magic yet.

While I was sleeping off my magical hangover and healing from a shot in the chest, Ezee had told Levi, Max, Rose, and Harper a pretty sensational account of my daring rescue. Harper and Levi were convinced I had a dire wolf familiar who could turn invisible at will now. I didn't correct them.

He left out the part where I nommed down on a man's heart. I was grateful for that. I still didn't know how I felt about it.

When I mercy-killed the wolf in Bernie's lair, I had felt so much pain and regret and revulsion for what I had to do. My heart had felt like it was going to crawl out of my chest, and I wanted to scrub my hands clean of blood like Lady Macbeth every time I thought about him. It had been merciful. The right thing to do. I still felt awful and sick about it. Bernie's memories hadn't even provided names for his victims. He hadn't cared enough to learn them.

But when I thought about Bernie, about thrusting my power into his chest and the hot, chewy taste of his heart between my teeth, I felt nothing. Empty. And I knew I would make the same choice again if I had to. I could run the scene through my mind a hundred times and I knew I would always choose his death and my friend's lives. Always.

After three days, I made Max drive me home in my car. Levi followed us and took him back to the B&B. I wanted to be alone. To process. The twins and Harper told me they understood, but I could see a million questions in their eyes. Questions I'd have to find answers for eventually if I was going to stick around.

My duffle bag was still sitting on the floor of my shop. Waiting for me to run. I picked it up and took it into my apartment. I dropped it on the coffee table and slumped onto my couch.

Stay? Or go?

Things weren't different. Samir was still going to come for me. I wasn't ready. I was more powerful than I had been a week ago, thanks to Bernie's donation, but I was magically flabby. I couldn't even put a fight half as good as the one I'd given him twenty years before. Not yet.

Someone tapped lightly on my door. I hadn't heard footsteps, so I knew instantly who it was. One giant blond pain in the ass coming right up.

"It's open," I called out. I actually wanted to talk to Alek. He'd been in and out of the B&B over the weekend, but we'd never had a chance to be alone.

He closed the door behind him and smiled at me before detouring into my kitchen and setting down a bag on the counter. Garlic and soy sauce wafted over to me. It smelled like heaven.

"Is that Chinese I smell?" I asked, even though the bag that read *Lee's Magic Kitchen* on the front was kind of a dead giveaway. "You are a god among men."

"That's a much nicer greeting than you gave me the first time we met," he said. He came over and sat down on the couch beside me, close enough that his thigh touched mine. I didn't move away.

"Yeah, well, you weren't exactly nice either. I believe you called me a murderer." I frowned as I said it. I hadn't been one that day. I was definitely one now.

He studied me for a moment and then looked at my duffle bag. "Are you still leaving?"

"I don't know," I said. "I'm tired of running. And as much as it really, really kills me to admit you were right… well… you were right."

"What's that? I'm sorry, I think I dozed off for a moment." He was smirking again.

"My ex is still going to come for me," I said, ignoring his teasing. "I'm not ready."

He shrugged. "So get ready."

"It's not that simple. I'll have to start using my magic. A lot. Training. I don't even know where to begin. I should probably learn to use a gun, or how to fight, or maybe kung fu. I'm not cut out for this, and I probably don't have enough time before he shows up. He could be here tomorrow. Or in a year. I don't know. It's not simple," I repeated.

"Yes," he said, flipping to serious mode. "It is. I have been assigned to this region. The Nine want a Justice around here for a while. I can help you, if you'll let me."

"Even knowing what I am? Seeing what I did?" I bit my lower lip and held my breath. This was the conversation I wanted to have, but I dreaded it anyway.

"Two weeks ago, I was sent a dream by the Nine. In that dream I saw a beautiful woman with hair like smoke and eyes full of fire. A giant crow soared above her and on one side of her was a pile of corpses shrouded in shadows as far as my eye could see. On the other side there was a sea of woodland creatures who laughed and danced in a sunny meadow."

"I think the humans have psychotherapy that can help with that," I said, trying to diffuse the awkwardness I felt at his intense recounting.

"Hush," he said. "That woman was you, Jade Crow. But she was not you, also. That night, in the circle beneath the full moon, I saw you choose the sunlight, choose life. That is a strength I am happy to encourage. A woman I want to know."

Tears burned in my eyes. I was going to have to magically cauterize my tear ducts or something at this rate if I kept crying all the time.

"But I killed him," I said, curling my hands into fists in my lap. "And I don't feel bad about it. At all. I'd do it again. I *want* to do it again. To Samir. I want to rip his heart out and destroy him forever."

"Good." Alek wrapped his hands around mine and gently pried my fingers open, rubbing his thumbs over my palms. "Some people need killing. Not everyone deserves life. This is something they taught me at Justice Academy."

I squinted at him. "Wait, there's really a Justice Academy?"

He laughed, the sound deep and beautiful and clean. "No."

"Fucker," I muttered.

Then he kissed me. His lips were firm against mine and liquid desire raced from my mouth straight into my lady bits. I moaned as his tongue slid into my mouth and crawled into his lap as his hands wrapped around my back and tangled in my hair. After what felt like much too short a time, he pulled away. Looking into his eyes I saw only a warm summer-sky shade of blue—none of the glacial ice I'd always compared them to.

"The food will get cold," he murmured. "Do you care?"

"Yes," I said as my stomach growled in a very unsexy manner. "To be continued, okay?"

"If you are staying," he said, and I knew he meant more than just here, in this moment.

"Yes," I said. I could almost say it without feeling terrified.

"I like when you tell the truth," he said.

"I'm a work in progress." I pried myself off his lap. "Now we're gonna eat. And then you, mister, are going to play a video game with me."

"Oh?" He stood up and pulled me back against him, nuzzling my hair.

I could definitely get used to that. "Yep. I can't date a non-gamer. It's just not done. So we're going to have to shoot some bandits and save the Borderlands."

"I've never played a video game," he said.

"Don't worry," I teased. "I'll be gentle."

He bent down and bit my earlobe before whispering in Russian, "I won't."

His words turned my legs into Gumby imitations, but I managed to stagger away from him toward the kitchen, ducking my head so my hair fell in a curtain and covered my blushing face. I might have brown skin, but I was sure I was scarlet at that moment. This thing between Alek and I, whatever this was, it was new to me. I hadn't dated in years, choosing to keep my relationships in Wylde strictly friendship-based. After all, I really hadn't shown great judgment in choosing boyfriends before.

But here I was, about to share a meal with a sexy tiger shifter who knew what I was, knew the dangers I posed, and was still here. In my home. Not running.

I knew then that Alek was right, damn him. I was done just surviving. It was time to live.

If you want to be notified when Annie Bellet's next novel is released, please sign up for the mailing list by going to: http://tinyurl.com/anniebellet Your email address will never be shared and you can unsubscribe at any time.

Word of mouth and reviews are vital for any author to succeed. If you enjoyed the book, please consider leaving a review wherever you purchased it. Even a few lines sharing your thoughts on this story would be extremely helpful for other readers. Thank you!

Turn the page to read the first two chapters of *Murder of Crows*, the second book in *The Twenty-Sided Sorceress* series.

Murder of Crows

Chapter One

The battlefield was quiet in the summer sunlight. I heard only the hum of insects and a light shushing of wind. My back was sweaty where I pressed it against the bark of an oak, using the tree as cover from the enemy I couldn't see or hear, but knew was out there across the meadow. The pile of ammo at my feet had dwindled down to a double handful. In the shade of the trees to my right, Harper's brother Max lay prone, red dripping down his chest and staining the dead leaves beneath him.

To the other side of me, Alek crouched among slender aspen trees, his arm useless, his leg oozing colors, his gun on the ground. He gave me a Gallic shrug and slight smile, the afternoon breeze lifting his white-blond hair off his forehead, his ice-blue eyes glinting with dark humor.

A paintball burst on a tree trunk just over his head.

"So," he said. "We're outmanned and outgunned."

"Maybe you should untie my hands," I said.

"That's not the point of the game," Max pointed out.

"For a corpse, you are doing a lot of talking." I glared at the kid, but he just grinned.

Peeking around the tree, I surveyed the meadow. Ezee's body was a dark lump in the grass. He was the only one I'd brought down so far, no thanks to the "help" on my team. I was pretty damn sure Alek and Max had gotten shot on purpose so that I'd have to figure out how to take down Harper and Ezee's twin, Levi, on my own.

We were gathered on this lovely summer Sunday out at The Henhouse Bed and Breakfast, where Harper and Max's mother Rosie was letting us train. Three months ago, I'd saved her from an evil warlock, but exposed myself to an old rival. A man who would come after me.

Kind of surprising he hadn't already, really. Samir, my psychokiller ex, had restrained himself to sending cryptic postcards and had yet to show his face. I knew he would tire of sending messages and show up eventually.

I needed to get my sorceress powers stronger before that happened. Much, much stronger.

Hence the paintball game of ultimate unfairness. Ezee, Harper, and Levi were all accomplished paintballers as well as shape shifters, which meant they got super speed, strength, extraordinary senses, and great reaction time to go with their crack-shot abilities, and they were on the opposing side. That left me with Alek, who should have been good at paintball since he could shoot real guns just fine, and Max, who was more enthusiastic than skilled. Sure, my team were shifters also, and yet here they were, out of the game already without more than a couple shots fired.

Leaving me, with my hands literally tied behind my back, to somehow win this thing. Magically. No gun. No hands. Just power. But the rules said I had to win by hitting my opponents with paintballs, so I couldn't just wrap a shield around myself and go hunt them down that way. No shields allowed today, either.

They'd taken away all my fun. By "fun," I do mean crutches. Bastards.

A green ball splattered on the tree trunk behind me.

"Best two out of three?" I yelled.

Another paintball, this one orange, smacked into the tree, misting paint onto my nose.

"Guess that's a no," I muttered as I wiped my nose on my shoulder as best I could.

"Perhaps if you sit here all day, they will get bored and come to you," Alek said. He pulled a knife from his boot, using its point to pick at his fingernails.

I considered telling him where to stick that knife but decided to concentrate on how I was going to win this thing. I looked around the tree again. The meadow sloped slightly downhill toward the thicket of saplings and brush where Harper and Levi were holed up. They couldn't cross the meadow, as Ezee's suspiciously snoring body demonstrated, but neither could I go to them. I couldn't even see them down there and I knew they'd be able to see me much clearer with their supernaturally enhanced senses.

If only my spirit guardian, the wolflike creature I creatively called Wolf, was useful for this shit. She was lounging in the shade deeper into the trees in which I was currently hiding, her tufted ears perked as I glared at her and she swished her long and thick black tail. Wolf could only help me with magical attacks and problems. Not that she would help here anyway. She seemed to understand this was all play and was content to watch. Traitor.

I twisted my arms a bit, testing the orange baling twine's knots. They weren't tied that tight—the purpose wasn't to really restrain me but to keep me from using gestures to help me cast spells. I was much better at casting when I could use my hands to direct energy. It was another crutch. Truly great magic shouldn't need hands. I needed my brain to be able to think outside the normal physical limitations of the world.

It's easy to pick up a couple rocks or paintballs with magic when you can just extend it as a gesture your body and mind are already used to. But visualizing having three or four or five hands? Tougher. The human brain isn't used to being able to lift five things at once in all directions. In order to get my brain to do it, I had to break reality a little, starting in my thoughts.

Break reality. I clung to that thought. I had been flinging paintballs at them like I was the gun, but there was really no need to do so. I didn't need to conform to the physics of a gun when I threw. I could be like that one cheesy movie where they bent bullets and stuff.

Theoretically.

"You aren't dead," I whispered to Alek, "so get ready to help." I didn't have super senses, but I had someone who did.

Alek's leg and arm had been hit, but he wasn't technically out, though he couldn't shoot anymore. That was okay; I didn't need his gun. I needed the tiger in him, his keen hunter's senses and instincts. He was a freakin' Justice, the shifter equivalent of Robocop, basically. Judge, jury, and sometimes executioner. He should be able to handle a little long-distance reconnaissance.

"What do you need?" he whispered back.

I told him. He started to laugh, but choked it back and nodded.

I dropped down carefully to make room by the oak trunk for Alek, keeping my profile as low as possible. I closed my eyes and visualized the thicket Harper and Levi were hiding in. I heard the slight shift of clothing as Alek crept up to the tree I'd been hiding behind, felt his warmth as he crouched against my body. I was almost sad Max was lying right there, because suddenly I could think of a lot more interesting things to be doing in the woods on a warm summer day.

Okay, focus. Paintball. Not licking Alek's chin and begging for kisses. Yeah.

I opened my eyes, keeping the image of the thicket in my mind as I looked down at the small pile of paintballs. One of the exercises I do, the only one I kept doing in my twenty-five years of running and hiding from Samir, was to lift multiple stones and form patterns into the air. The paintballs weren't much different than the stones. About the same size, a little lighter.

Usually, however, I had my hands to help me visualize things. I couldn't even grab my talisman, the silver twenty-sided die around my neck, for a focus.

I summoned my power, letting it stream through me in a shivering rush, and lifted one paintball, then another, and another, until all eight remaining were in the air. I sent them up through the trees, as high as I could without losing my thin tether of magic and control. I just hoped I could stretch my magic across the meadow. Too late now to back out of the plan. If this didn't work, I'd have to surrender. No more ammo.

"Ready?" Alek whispered.

I nodded, not trusting speech.

Alek whipped his head out from behind the tree, squinting down the field, his eyes probably picking out details in the shifting shadows of the thicket that I would never know.

A paintball burst on the tree by his head; another whizzed by and splattered on the next tree in.

"Send the balls, I know where they are," he whispered.

I sent my paintballs, still high up in the air, down the left of the field, hoping they would be far out of Harper and Levi's lines of sight. Alek looked around the tree again, this time from the other side.

"Harper is behind that bush with the dark green and white leaves. Levi is crouched behind those two saplings with the twinned trunks."

I peeked around the tree, picking out where he'd said they were. I saw nothing but slight movement in the leaves of the bush which could have been wind. If Alek was wrong, we'd lose.

Fortunately, in the three months I'd been sharing my bed with him, I'd learned that Alek wasn't wrong very often. And he hated losing almost as much as I did.

In my mind, I gathered the paintballs into two groups of four, pushing on my magic to send one group over the bush where Harper was and the other group around behind the saplings. Their foliage wasn't thick, the trees too young to have many branches. I guess Harper and Levi hadn't thought about cover from above.

Rule number one of horror movies? No one ever looks up.

My magic was holding, though it felt like I had dragged hot wires out of my brain and my power was slippery in my mental grasp. I could see the thin tethers holding the balls in the air, which meant another sorcerer would be able to as well. I filed that information away.

"Geronimo," I said under my breath as I pooled more magic around the balls and shoved them downward as hard as my weakening control would allow.

"Fuck!"

"Holy shitballs!"

The exclamations from the thicket were music to my ears.

Harper and Levi stood up from their spots, their heads and shoulders running with a rainbow of paint colors. In the meadow, Ezee sat up and started laughing.

"You two look like a unicorn took a shit on you," Max yelled, getting to his feet.

"Frag the weak! Hurdle the dead!" I yelled, heaving to my feet and running out into the meadow. I used a bit of power to burn away the baling twine on my wrists and thrust my sore arms out, making airplane noises as I ran in a circle through the grass.

"What are you, an Argentinean soccer player?" Ezee said, still laughing. He brushed at his khaki shorts, though there was nothing to be done about the splatters of paint. Somehow he made them look artsy and cool. Ezee could make any outfit look nice.

"*Futbol*, not soccer. Geez," I said, grinning.

Paint exploded onto my chest, the balls stinging madly as they burst. I fell backward into the grass.

"Hey," I said as Harper stalked toward me. "I won, no fair."

"Mom has tea ready. Let's go get cleaned up." Harper stuck her tongue out at me and walked toward the large house in the distance.

"Sorry," Levi called out. "Can't trust a fox, eh? Good job with dropping those balls on us, by the way." He offered a hand to his brother and they followed after Harper.

"If only Harper felt the same way," I muttered. "Somebody is a sore loser."

Alek swept me up into his arms and kissed my forehead. "Takes one to know one, eh?"

Laughing, covered in paint and tired as hell, I pushed him away and followed the others to the house. Another lesson learned, I guess.

I wasn't laughing later when we got back to my place. Alek was still mostly living in his little trailer, which he'd parked out at the B&B at Rosie's invitation, but we spent a lot of nights at my apartment above my game and comics store.

My mail was stuffed in the box by my back door, and I saw the postcard even as I picked up the slim pile. Another missive from Samir. Awesome.

"Want me to burn it?" Alek asked as I set the mail on my kitchen table and picked up the postcard.

"No, safer to keep them in the iron box behind wards," I said. Alek was the only one I had told about the postcards, mostly because he'd been there when the first arrived in the mail a mere week after the mess with the warlock.

This one was like the others, only my address and name on it, no message. Just a stylized S. Creepy fucker. The first had been of the Eiffel Tower in Paris. The next showed up a couple weeks later and had a picture of a canal in Venice. The third was another three weeks after that with a bunch of castle ruins from some place in Scotland.

This was the fourth. It was just a photo of a bunch of trees, no small text on the back telling me where it was taken. It looked weirdly familiar, however. I pushed away the shiver that crept over my skin. There were conifer forests like that all over the world. No reason to think it was from around here.

"Sometimes I wish he'd just show up and get this over with," I muttered. I didn't really. Samir would crush me. I was getting stronger, but I had no illusions that I could beat a sorcerer who'd been around since the days when Brutus stabbed a guy named Caesar.

"Every minute he doesn't is good for you," Alek said. "You did well today; you are getting stronger, learning new ways to control your powers."

I smiled up at him. He always somehow knew the right thing to say, even if sometimes I wanted to punch him in the face for saying uncomfortable truths. It was Alek who had postulated that Samir hadn't shown up yet because he was uncertain of me. Alek had a point. I had gone dark for twenty-five years, running and hiding and barely using magic. Samir had almost caught up to me a couple times, but I'd slipped away from him and stayed hidden.

Until three months ago. Then I'd blazed onto the magical map. Alek pointed out that I'd appeared here, near the River of No Return wilderness which had one of the strongest networks of ley lines running beneath its millions of unbroken wild acreage, and living in a town full of shape shifters and other magical beings. From Samir's perspective, this whole thing probably looked like some kind of trap. Why else would I stop hiding if I weren't ready for him, right?

Alek's logic made a certain kind of sense. Samir was arrogant enough to believe his calculated approach to life was the way anyone would approach things. He wasn't the type to risk his life for anyone, so he would never understand or conceive of the choice I'd made three months ago. I could have stayed hidden, but friends would have died, and I would have had to leave the life I'd built here.

I was done running. Hence the whole training to use my powers and pretending that if I did, I could win against Samir.

I knew I couldn't. But I didn't have the heart to tell Alek or Harper or the twins that. They believed in me; the least I could do was try to go down fighting when the time came.

"I'm taking a shower," I said. "Joining me?"

"No," Alek said with regret in his voice. "I'm going to try calling Carlos again." His handsome brow creased in worry. It was Sunday, which meant he usually called and talked to his mentor and friend, a fellow Justice named

Carlos. It had been two weeks since Carlos and he had talked, however, and Alek was worried. I hoped he reached him tonight. A Justice going silent was probably not a good sign.

I came out into the living room after showering the last of the paint out of my waist-length black hair and cuddled up to Alek on the couch. I knew from the worry in his blue eyes even before I asked that he hadn't reached Carlos.

"Nothing?"

"No," he said, sliding an arm around my shoulders. "Nothing."

"Wouldn't the Council tell you if there was something to worry about?" I leaned into him, tucking my head against his broad chest, and breathed in his vanilla-musk scent.

"Perhaps," he said softly. He shook his head and took a steadying breath. "I called for pizza while you were in the shower. Half all meat, half pepperoni and pineapple."

It was a sign of how comfortable we were getting with each other that he knew what to get me, especially considering he thought fruit on pizza was an abomination. I wasn't sure how I felt about that—the comfort level or the whole aversion to delicious pineapple.

"You still coming to game on Thursday? You aren't going to dodge it again, right? We're down a man 'cause Steve has that family thing." We'd been trying to get Alek to game with us for months. I'd broken him in to video games, but we'd yet to get dice into his hands.

He sighed. "I'll be there," he said, nuzzling my hair and sliding his hands under my teeshirt.

Which was when someone knocked on the door.

"Pizza!" Alek said, grinning as I pushed my teeshirt back down.

"I'm gonna kill that guy for his timing," I muttered.

Alek opened the door, but it wasn't the pizza man. Instead a tall, wiry man stood there, his eyes sunken and tired-looking in his nut-brown face, but his irises were still the moss green I remembered and his thick black hair was still cropped close to his skull. Just as it had been when I'd last seen him, over thirty years before.

When he told me I was dead to the tribe. When he kicked me out of my home for good.

"Jade," the man said, looking uncertainly past Alek.

"Alek," I said. "Would you kindly slam the door in my father's face?"

Chapter Two

Alek didn't end up slamming the door. The pizza guy chose that moment to show up, causing a shuffle of people as we paid him and sent him away, which ended up with all of us standing awkwardly in my kitchen.

"What are you doing here, Jasper?" I asked, emphasizing his name. He didn't get to be called Dad anymore. "How did you even find me?"

My anger wasn't pretty. It burned through me, threatening to boil over, and my magic sang in my veins as I struggled not to do something regrettable. I had thought my resentment, anger, and grief long dead. Guess I was wrong about that. I didn't think Alek would let me blast my father out of existence, however, even if I had truly wanted to. Alek was a Justice and supposed to protect shifters. Dear old Dad was a crow shifter. QED and all that jazz.

"I hired a private investigator," Jasper said. He glanced at Alek, who was wisely standing by my side and keeping his mouth shut for the moment. "I didn't expect to find you so close to home."

"This is my home." My father looked smaller and older than I remembered but I knew it was likely time and memory playing tricks on me. I'd been all of fourteen and just a kid the last time I saw him. He was still taller than I, his face mostly unlined in that ageless way older shifters had, where he could be anywhere from thirty-five to fifty depending on expression and lighting.

"Jade," he said, softly this time, his green eyes full of a desperate fire. "I need your help."

I laughed. I couldn't stop it from coming out, the hysterical giggles turning into full-blown gasping laughter.

"Go fuck yourself," I said. "And get the fuck out of my house."

"Jade," Alek said, placing a hand on my shoulder. His touch was steadying, even if it pissed me off a little more.

"You stay out of this." I looked up at him as I gained control of my laughter. "That man kicked me out, they all did. Sent me away to live with a woman who was little better than a slave master and her rapist husband. You know the last words that man spoke to me?" I pointed at Jasper. " 'You are dead to the People. You must go away from here and never return.' So don't you go feeling sorry for him."

I hadn't discussed that part of my life with Alek. He knew I'd been on the street, knew about my real family, the four nerds who took me in when I was a teenager and raised me until Samir killed them. I hadn't told Alek about the People. They were a dead part of my life.

"Does Granddaddy Crow know you are here?" I asked Jasper. I figured the old bastard who led the cult that was my former tribe would know. No one did anything without Sky Heart's say-so.

"Sky Heart does not know," Jasper said. "I have come to you on my own. We are desperate."

That surprised me. The Crow who were my former people weren't anything like the Crow tribe, the Apsaalooké, who lived in Montana and were mostly human. Jasper's Crow were crow shifters, exclusively. Back in the early seventeen hundreds, Sky Heart, a crow shifter and warrior of the actual Crow people, decided crow shifters were special and should live apart. He took a group of them, gathered from many tribes, and went west to finally settle in what became northern Washington state, at a thousand acre forested parcel of land he named Three Feathers. To guard the people and shore up his own power, Sky Heart summoned a powerful spirit, who called itself Shishishiel, the Crow, and from there on out gathered only crow shifters to him. Which involved some fairly underhanded shit like stealing crow shifters from other places, killing those who didn't want to come live with the People, and, oh yeah, kicking out any children who didn't turn into crows.

So, you know, typical cult. I hadn't realized it when I'd been in it, of course. It wasn't until years later when I talked it over with my adopted family that I had seen how dysfunctional they really were. Before that, all I knew was that I was different and had to leave.

"The pizza is getting cold," Alek said. His stomach rumbled.

"So eat it," I said. "Jasper is leaving."

"I cannot leave," Jasper said. "Just please hear me out."

"It cannot hurt to hear him out." Alek turned those big blue eyes of his on me and I sighed.

So we ended up sitting around the kitchen table, Alek eating his pizza, me picking at a slice of mine, and Jasper clutching the glass of water Alek had offered him like it was the last piece of floating wood in a shipwreck.

Part of me wanted to break the ice and ask how Pearl, my mother, was. But I resisted. This man didn't deserve a lifeline like that, and nor did either he or my mother deserve my interest or concern.

Finally, after long enough that the awkwardness in the air was as congealed at the cheese on my pizza, Jasper spoke.

"Someone, or something, is killing off the People," he said. "Sky Heart promises he and Shishishiel can stop it, but I think he lies. He says that it is because we have grown too weak, too easy on our young, our blood too diluted with crows who are not Natives. I do not believe this is so."

"You are half white," I pointed out. "Wasn't it Sky Heart who brought in your mother? He is the one who tracks down crow shifters from all over North America and forces them to join you, so he'd be the one to blame if your so-called blood is getting too impure." The whole thing disgusted me. Ruby, my grandmother, had died before I was born, sometime back around World War Two, but my mother had told me about her, about how Sky Heart kept her imprisoned in his home until she bore him a son who changed into a crow. She was where my father got his green eyes.

"Yes," he said, not meeting my gaze. "This is a reason I do not believe. There is magic at work. These murders are not natural. Someone is killing us off and no one will act."

Magic. Samir. No, that would be too easy. If he was killing off my former family to get to me, he'd be gloating more about it. And my father wouldn't be standing here talking to me. He'd be dead.

"Is Pearl alive?" I asked.

"Yes, your mother is fine. But without magic of our own to stop the killing..." He trailed off, eyes still fixed on the water droplets condensing on his glass.

So, not Samir. I took a deep breath. It wouldn't, shouldn't, matter if it were. I wasn't going to help the people who had declared me dead and cast me out.

"What makes you think I have magic that can help you?" I kept staring at him, hard. When I had left, my powers were barely anything. I could occasionally move things with my mind when I was really upset, but that was about it. It wasn't until a couple years later, with the help of my new family and some Dungeons & Dragons manuals to act as focuses, that I'd begun to really work magic.

Jasper raised his head. "Because of what you are," he said. "Because of who your father is."

My chair hit the floor as I jerked to my feet. This was like a bad parody of *Star Wars*. "My… father? You were my father." I made sure, even in my shock, to keep to the past tense. My chest hurt, as though bands were tightening inside my ribs, making it hard to breathe. Alek rose and picked up my chair, gently pushing on my shoulders until I sat again.

"No. Your mother left us for a while, many years ago." Jasper took a few deep breaths and continued. "After Ruby died, she was unhappy with the People."

"So she escaped," I said. I shrugged Alek's hands off my shoulders. I wished he would leave in the same moment that I was glad he was there. Someone needed to witness the total crazy, I guess.

"Yes," Jasper said the word like it pained him. "She was pregnant when she came back. With you."

Came back? "Dragged back by Sky Heart and my father" was probably more accurate if I had to guess, but there was no point asking.

"So who is my father?"

"I do not know," Jasper said. He held up a hand to stall my exasperated exclamation. "Your mother says he was a powerful sorcerer. She was sure you inherited his powers. Even as a baby when you were angry we saw things shift and move. Do you not have powers?"

I didn't know if I was relieved by this news. Not being related to the asshole in front of me was sort of nice, but it left me with more questions. And a horrible fear.

"Did Pearl say what this man looked like? Was he Native American at least?" I prayed Jasper would say yes. *Universe please, let him say yes.*

"Yes," he said, and the lump in my throat lessened. "She has said that much. You are full blood, if that worried you." There was bitterness in his tone.

I almost explained. It wasn't that I cared if I had white or whatever blood in me. It was that Samir wasn't Native and for a terrible moment I'd feared that I'd been lovers with my own father. It would have made a horrible kind of sense and be just the sort of twisted, fucked-up shit Samir would pull.

I didn't owe Jasper any explanations, so I kept quiet about why I'd asked. Alek's considering stare told me he had guessed my reasoning behind the question. I figured there were some awkward conversations we'd have to have later. Much, much later. After I got Jasper out of my house.

"Shifters are dying?" Alek asked, turning his piercing gaze on Jasper. "Has the Council sent someone?" The Council of Nine was a guardian and governing body for shifters, though no one really knew much about them, not even Alek, who worked for them. The Nine were practically shifter gods, there but not exactly reachable by phone.

"They did, though Sky Heart does not recognize the Nine. A man showed up after the third murder. Our leader had words with him, then the Justice left."

I watched Alek's face as he seemed to do some mental math and that sinking feeling started up again in my stomach.

"This Justice, was he a white man?" Alek asked.

"No, black. A huge man, I think a lion shifter from how he smelled. Sky Heart was very angry with him."

Alek moved from the side of the table to loom over Jasper. "When did you see the Justice last?" His tone was intense as he bit off each syllable, his hands clenched into fists at his sides.

"A week ago? No, a little more. It was Friday, I think, so eight or nine days. Why?"

Alek pulled his silver feather talisman that marked him as a Justice out from under his shirt. Jasper's eyes widened but an excited expression came over him.

"Good, you can help as well. We need both of you. Shifters being murdered is Council business, no? No matter what Sky Heart says." His eyes flicked between us.

"The Justice who showed up," Alek said. "His name is Carlos." He looked at me. "I have to go contact the Council."

"What about Jasper?" I said. I knew that this might be Justice business, now that Carlos was involved, but no way was this man staying in my home a minute longer than necessary.

"He will come with me," Alek said after a moment. He smiled, his face sympathetic, and I couldn't decide if I wanted to punch him or kiss him. That happens to me a lot with Alek.

"You will consider helping, Jade?" Jasper rose as Alek stepped back, giving him space again.

"No," I said and pretended that the look of despair on his face didn't tug any heartstrings. "This is Justice business. They can deal with it."

It was a lie. I knew that if Alek asked me instead of Jasper, I'd go help. Maybe. My wounds weren't healed even after thirty-three years and I wasn't sure I wanted to rip off the bandages. My past was better left in the past.

Alek and Jasper moved toward the door.

"I'll call you or come by tomorrow, yes?" Alek said.

"Okay," I said, leaning up to give him a kiss. I made sure to put tongue in it, hoping it would make Jasper uncomfortable. Guess I'm petty like that.

"Wait," I called after them as they were halfway down the stairs. "How many murders?" I asked Jasper.

"Eleven," he said, his lips pressing into a white line and his expression going flat in a way I remembered from when I was a kid, a flatness that said there was too much emotion beneath for him to handle.

Eleven. When I'd left Three Feathers, there had been about a hundred Crow living there. I closed the door and slid down it to the floor.

Guess it was a good thing I'm a Band-Aid-fast kind of girl, because I knew in my heart that no matter what Alek found out or what his Council said, I was going back to Three Feathers and the People.

Want to read the rest? Look for *Murder of Crows* at all major retailers or go here http://overactive.wordpress.com/twenty-sided-sorceress/ for links and more information.

Also by Annie Bellet:

The Gryphonpike Chronicles:

Witch Hunt

Twice Drowned Dragon

A Stone's Throw

Dead of Knight

The Barrows (Omnibus Vol.1)

Chwedl Duology:

A Heart in Sun and Shadow

The Raven King

Pyrrh Considerable Crimes Division Series:

Avarice

Short Story Collections:

The Spacer's Blade and Other Stories

River Daughter and Other Stories

Deep Black Beyond

Till Human Voices Wake Us

Dusk and Shiver

Forgotten Tigers and Other Stories

About the Author:

Annie Bellet lives and writes in the Pacific NW. She is the author of the *Gryphonpike Chronicles* and the *Twenty-Sided Sorceress* series, and her short stories have appeared in over two dozen magazines and anthologies. Follow her on her blog at "A Little Imagination".

http://overactive.wordpress.com/

Printed in Poland
by Amazon Fulfillment
Poland Sp. z o.o., Wrocław